The Necessities of Life

The Necessities of Life

BY

ED FORD

Acclaim Press
MORLEY, MISSOURI

P.O. Box 238
Morley, MO 63767
(573) 472-9800
www.acclaimpress.com

Book & Cover Design: Frene Melton

ISBN: 978-1-956027-32-7 | 1-956027-32-7
Library of Congress Control Number: 2022940400

First Printing: 2022
Printed in the United States of America
10 9 8 7 6 5 4 3 2 1

CONTENTS

DEDICATION

To the teachers of the world, men and women who have dedicated their lives to preparing us to be the best that we can be.

ACKNOWLEDGMENTS

The Necessities of Life is based on the lifetime experience of Ruby Robinson Ford and Carl G. Ford. Interviews with them provided the basis for this story, a positive account about the values of education and the people of Eastern Kentucky.

History professor Dr. Paul Rominger also was a major contributor concerning the life and times of those experiencing the hardships of the Great Depression.

Author Shirley Baechtold and Dr. Wilma (Willi) Walker, respected college professors, suggested improvements that were essential. Longtime Madison County Attorney Marc Robbins was a great legal source, and, as always, IT authority Roy Varney led the way to publication.

The Necessities of Life

CHAPTER ONE

DEPARTURE

Dad was dying. He knew it and I knew it, but it didn't warrant a lengthy discussion.

We'd found out about the cancer right after Christmas when the family doctor checked Dad for what he thought was a virus. A few x-rays and blood tests later, the problem was pinpointed. It wasn't good news.

"I want you to see an oncology specialist," Dr. Thomas told Dad. "Dinesh Hashmeer is one of the best in the state. He's Indian by birth and southern by culture," he smiled, "so don't let the Bombay body with a Birmingham accent throw you."

Dr. Hashmeer, who was the size of a National Football League linebacker, told Dad the malignancy was in the liver. And, he wanted to operate. After a few minutes of discussion, Dad agreed.

The surgery was scheduled at the university hospital in Lexington. When the day of action arrived, I caught a glimpse of the doctor as Dad was being wheeled into surgery and was surprised when, a short time later, Hashmeer came by the waiting room to see me.

"You're a fast worker," I grinned. But Hashmeer wasn't smiling.

"He's eaten up with cancer," he said. "It's multiplying like crazy—much worse than I thought. Surgery won't help. We just closed the incision and sent him to recovery."

It took a moment for the news to sink in. Mom had died three years ago and I wasn't prepared for Dad to follow this soon.

"Your father is suffering from cholangiocarcinoma, also known as bile duct cancer. Basically, it's considered incurable and has a very rapid lethal rate. If he had just one tumor we might have some options. But, his liver is eaten up with them. His condition is too advanced for us to do anything other then providing medication that will make him more comfortable."

"How long does he have?" I asked.

Hashmeer shrugged his shoulders and rubbed the back of his neck.

"It's really hard to tell. Maybe two or three months, maybe longer. He's pretty tough, so he may surprise us."

"A year?" I questioned.

Hashmeer shook his head.

"I think you should be the one to tell him," he said. "He'll take it better knowing that you know."

Dad was my idol, my anchor. As a youngster, I was convinced there was no better man alive than my father. His father, my grandfather, had died when Dad—John Martin Graybeal Graham—was two years old. Gray, as Dad was called, was reared in Eastern Kentucky's Shawnee County by his mother and two sets of grandparents who lived within a stone's throw of each other. They laid out a strict path for him to follow—to be honest, hard-working and to do what was right. And, to be the first in both families to get a college education.

The Depression had made finances meager, but everyone—including Dad—would work hard to make a bachelor's degree possible. And, his two grandfathers emphasized self-reliance and to handle difficult situations head-on.

"You've got to be tough," his grandfathers had said. "If you're backed against the wall and there's no alternative, fight your way out!"

Not surprisingly, those same principles were passed down to me, John Colliver Graham. They call me Jack.

Dad's Scots-Irish heritage served him well. He got his college degree in secondary education in the early 1930s and went to work as a teacher. He was good, well respected and had exceptional leadership skills. Money was tight and moving up the educational ladder depended upon timing and a lot of good luck. But, he had done it, serving as a high school principal and superintendent before becoming a university professor.

But now, his retirement years were facing immediate closure.

The next afternoon Dad walked a bit and sat up in a comfortable high-backed chair next to his hospital bed. I pulled a chair in front of him and cleared my throat.

"I need to tell you something," I began.

"No need," he said, leaning his head back against the padded cushion. He squinted his eyes and ran his tongue over his dry lips. "I have a feeling the surgery wasn't successful."

"How do you know?" I asked.

"Just a feeling," he replied. "When I was in recovery, the door to my room was open and I could see the wall clock in the hallway. I wasn't in surgery long enough. My guess is that the cancer is extensive."

I dropped my head, a dead giveaway that he was right.

"How long do I have?"

"The surgeon says not long. Maybe two or three months."

I looked him in the eyes.

"How do you want to handle this? We can ask for another opinion, try to find a solution or maybe just do something you'd like to do. What do you think?"

Dad paused, then had a faraway look in his eyes.

"Let's go back to Citation."

CHAPTER TWO

BOWMAN

"You okay, Dad?"

My father took a deep breath and nodded.

"Yeah, I'm fine. Just stay on this road and follow the creek. There's a bridge somewhere up ahead that leads into Citation."

Citation. The name was a synonym for achievement, an honor or an award. In the 1930s, it identified a location that was designed to be the best coal mining operation in Southeastern Kentucky. Beneath the beautiful green-clad mountains lay a fortune in bituminous coal. But getting to Citation was a 200-mile journey from our Central Kentucky homes. It was a comfortable drive, however, as the traffic was manageable and the late May weather was warm and everything was in bloom.

"Everything has changed," Dad noted. "I know we're on the right path, but I can't believe all the trees and undergrowth. You used to be able to see the coal tipple from here."

I grinned.

"That was fifty years ago, Dad. I must have been about four or five when we lived in Citation and you were in your late twenties."

"Twenty-eight," he said. "That was in thirty-eight, just before the war. You were just a baby when we drove up here. Your mother thought we were lost. She'd never been in Eastern Kentucky before and only knew about Shawnee County from what I'd told her."

Dad chuckled as he recollected.

"She said it was the most God-forsaken area she'd ever seen and if there wasn't a better teaching job here we might as well turn around, hope for the best, and head home."

My thoughts turned to my mother, Martha. She was a great mom, good looking, intelligent, musically talented and could adapt to nearly every situation, good or bad. She was tall—about 5-foot-8—and was a great match for my rugged father. In his prime, Dad stood just under six feet and was a muscular one-hundred ninety pounds.

When mom was pregnant with me she had a rough time. She was in labor for twenty-four hours and, after I was born, she learned she could never have any more children. Unfazed, she told Dad that their work was cut out for them.

"We have to make this boy the very best he can be," she declared.

I was exposed to everything from athletics to good music and literature and was led down a path designed for success. I earned degrees in journalism, wrote for newspapers and magazines, married and had a son and a daughter and now was teaching journalism on the college level. Classes and exams were completed and this was a good time to visit Citation.

Teaching, I guess, was genetically ingrained in me. Mom, Martha Colliver Graham, had two years of normal school and was qualified to teach on the elementary and secondary levels. However, she had her hands full with me and was content to let her husband handle the educational chores. Jobs were scarce, and this coal company school was seeking a principal. Plus, the job came with a residence and dining facilities in the company clubhouse. It was too good an opportunity to let pass.

"My Uncle Bill Buck called me about the job," Dad continued. "He was sheriff of Shawnee County, knew the Princess Citation Mine manager and wanted me to interview for the job before the nephew of the county judge got his foot in the door."

"What did the mine manager have to do with it?" I asked.

"The Citation school was owned by the company and controlled by the coal company officials," Dad explained. "The mine manager, and sometimes the company officers, interviewed, hired and paid the teachers. And their schools generally were better than those in close-by communities operated by the county. Remember, when you control the purse strings you have the power and influence."

"So, you interviewed with the coal officials?" I questioned.

"Right. I met with Liam McLeod, who was the mine supervisor and manager of Princess Citation. Selkirk Coal and Coke out of Pittsburgh owned the mine and McLeod was their employee."

"LOOK OUT!" Dad cried.

I slammed on the brakes as a man wielding a machete walked from the underbrush and into the path of the car. The vehicle skidded to the side of the road and fishtailed toward the alarmed pedestrian, causing him to fall.

I jumped from the car, but halted when the man struggled to his feet and raised his machete in an offensive manner.

"Omigosh!" I cried as he stepped away. "Did I hit you? Are you okay?"

Lowering his "weapon," the man wiped his mouth with a shirtsleeve and glared at me.

"Who in the hell are you and what in the hell are you doing?" he shouted.

He reached down and picked up his cap, a dark blue baseball headpiece with an orange Old English D. I immediately recognized it as a Detroit Tigers cap.

"I'm on my way to the old Citation coal camp with my Dad," I said. "Are you sure you're alright?"

The "assailant" stared into the car and pointed the machete.

"Is that your Dad?"

I nodded yes.

"Tell him to get out of the car."

I hesitated. If there were going to be a confrontation I didn't want Dad to be part of it. But Dad already had opened his door.

"I know you!" the machete-wielder snapped as Dad stepped onto the pavement.

He glared as recognition surfaced.

"You're the Citation principal who blistered my ass with a paddle."

"Maybe," Dad acknowledged. "If I did, you deserved it. What's your name."

"Bowman, Darnell Bowman. I was in high school with Jimmy Dan Trivette and Little Bull Elliott. You whipped me for fighting in Mrs. Spurlock's class."

"Yeah, I remember," Dad replied. "Carol Ann had all kinds of problems with you."

"You called me up in front of the class and laid it to me. I told Little Bull that I'd get you for that. One day I'd get even."

"But you didn't. Why not?" Dad asked.

Bowman paused, slowly relaxed then broke out laughing.

"Because you were tougher than a pine knot. We were always a little bit afraid of you. Little Bull said you were Hell on Wheels.

"Looking back, I don't think you paddled anybody who didn't deserve it. And, you were a damned good teacher. I'll always remember that day we talked about the necessities of life. You talked about the importance of a good foundation and using it to build a good life. You made us learn and pushed us to do better. And you did it with a bunch of stubborn hard-headed coal mining kids."

Darnell tightened his grip on the machete and approached Dad. Minus a weapon, I might not be able to stop him. But I was ready to intervene.

"Going to get even with me now?" Dad asked. "I caution you. Be sure you can finish what you start. I may be a lot older, but, like you said, I'm tougher than a pine knot."

Gray widened his stance and balled his hands into fists. Darnell stopped within arms length and shifted the machete to his left hand.

"You're a hard man, but you made a difference. Would you shake my hand?"

CHAPTER THREE

REMNANTS

I backed the car onto the roadway and Dad got in with Bowman in the rear giving directions to the turnoff.

"Are you still living here?" Dad asked.

"No, I come down occasionally to check on some property I inherited. I live in Michigan now and get to Citation several times a year. I left here in forty-two and joined the Army as World War II was heating up. Jimmy Dan joined up with me and we fought in the European theater. I moved to Michigan and hired on at a Ford factory in Livonia after the war. J.D. came back here and reopened the old company store. It's the only thing left in the coal camp."

"Is it still open?" I questioned.

"Yeah and it does a good business. Jimmy Dan's son runs it now and gets customers from the junction and all over the southern part of the county. He sells everything from groceries to hardware to housing. James is a top-notch entrepreneur. His construction business probably brings in the most revenue.

"J.D. re-upped after the war and was in Korea, but he never made it back. He was one of the casualties at Pork Chop Hill."

Darnell placed his hand on my shoulder.

"Let me out here. The turnoff is about another mile just ahead. Turn left at the intersection and cross the bridge. Then it's welcome to Citation. At least, what's left of it."

Bowman fist-bumped Dad's shoulder as I stopped the car.

"Good to see you again, Mr. Graham. Don't know what you're looking for, but hope you won't be disappointed. I can remember some of the things that were here, but after Selkirk pulled out everything went to pot. Nature has a way of reclaiming the land."

"But not the memories," Dad smiled. "Thanks Darnell, good luck to you."

Bowman exited the car and waved as we departed.

"I don't remember this intersection," Dad commented as a stop sign came into view. "Guess that's another change."

The steel bridge also was relatively new and led directly to the railroad crossing. Beyond the tracks was a lone building bearing a sign—"Trivette Enterprises." A number of pickup trucks and autos were parked in front.

"That must be Jimmy Dan's place," I announced.

"That's it," Dad responded. "Sure doesn't look like the old company store."

Wheelbarrows, riding mowers and other equipment and implements ringed the exterior along with signs promoting their bargain prices. Gasoline pumps were nearby, followed by a two-lane road that ended just past the store.

"From this point it became a single-lane trail with a turn-around at its end," Dad explained. "All the roads were paved with cinders."

Dad was winded and removed a bottle of pills. He swallowed one with a drink from a water bottle.

"Let's sit here a minute until I get my bearings," he suggested.

He looked to the left and grinned.

"The company office was over to the left and another building to its right was a drug store, then a theater, some tennis courts and the clubhouse. And, a bank was just a little farther down."

"I thought a coal company town was pretty rough, but sounds like it wasn't all that bad," I said.

"The company built it well. It was really one of the better coal towns in Southeastern Kentucky. The miners' housing was on that little ridge to the right. The homes were all alike and side-by-side, but well built. Everything was close enough for the miners and their families to have walking access to the company store, drug store, theater and so forth. As I recall, there even was a barbershop farther down the road.

"The clubhouse had two floors with ten single family rooms and a bathroom at the end of the hall on the second floor. The downstairs housed a kitchen, a huge dining room and another bathroom. It really wasn't a bad situation.

"We lived in one of the rooms upstairs and a physician and a nurse also had rooms. All of us took our meals in the dining room and the food was good. I doubt that you can remember. You were too young."

"Where was the school?" I asked.

Dad looked past the miners' housing area and indicated a nearby road that paralleled the railroad tracks on one side and had a dense grove of trees on the other.

"Back up and take that road," he said.

I followed the indicated route and was told to stop at a clearing next to a gently sloping hillside. What appeared as part of an old foundation was at the base of the slope.

"This is it," Dad smiled. "Let's take a look around."

We stood at the base of the slope as Dad marked an outline of the building with the soles of his shoes. It took a while and, when finished, he had marked off an area of some 60x150 feet.

"Wow! That was a good-sized school," I exclaimed.

Dad nodded.

"The company built it with the help of the county the first year I was here. The school board pushed it through in a fall election, and the county boasted it was overseeing the construction as it was trying to get a foothold where control of the school was concerned. Most of the funding, however, came from Selkirk mining.

"This ended up as a first-class structure. It was a two-story frame building on a concrete slab. It had a huge auditorium with a stage on the first floor and seven classrooms, a library and my office on the second. We put up a basketball goal in front of the building, but the ground was so rocky it was impossible to dribble."

A nearby stone outcropping, however, provided a good place to sit and take a rest. Dad again was short of breath, but there was a gleam in his eyes indicating there was more to come.

"I have a feeling you're just getting warmed up," I smiled. "What else do you remember?"

Dad swabbed his face with a handkerchief.

"I've just laid the foundation," he said. "Most of what comes next you couldn't have known and, now, you won't believe it."

I could see his thoughts were returning to the thirties.

CHAPTER FOUR

McLEOD

Early August 1938

Graybeal Graham shifted gears as he slowly crossed the railroad tracks and spied the sign. It contained two lines: "Princess Citation Mine" on top and "Selkirk Coal and Coke Company" below.

He stopped in front of the larger building and saw an extraordinarily beautiful young woman standing at the entrance. She wore a nurses' uniform and was organizing several sheets of paper.

Gray exited the car and walked toward her, removing his hat as he approached.

"Pardon me. Could you tell me where I might find Mr. McLeod, the mine manager?"

She looked up from her paperwork and smiled. Her blue eyes and dazzling smile were framed by dark wavy hair. A white nurses cap sat atop her head.

"He's next door," she replied. "I was just going to his office. Join me and we'll walk over together."

She was of medium height and had an incredible figure.

"I'm Eileen Branscomb," she said. "I'm the nurse here at Princess Citation. Are you an acquaintance of Mr. McLeod?"

"No, but I hope to be more than an acquaintance. I'm seeing him about a job. I'm a teacher. My name is Graham, Gray Graham," he smiled and nodded.

"We have a nice school here," Eileen said. "I think you'll fit right in."

"Maybe I should interview with you. You make it sound like I'm already hired."

The nurse laughed.

"I'm been told that I'm a good judge of character. You look like a teacher—a good one."

"Thanks, that's quite a compliment. And, pardon me if I seem too forward. You look like..."

"I know," she again laughed. "Hedy Lamarr, the actress. They showed one of her movies at the theater last week and I was embarrassed by all the comments and attention."

Gray opened the door for Eileen as they reached McLeod's office. There were several chairs in a small lobby fronting a compact room with an open door. The occupant sat behind a worn wooden desk covered by several stacks of paperwork.

"Excuse me, Mr. McLeod," Eileen announced. "I have some information for you on some of the patients that Dr. Bradbury has seen. And, I have Mr. Graham who's here to see you."

Liam (Mac) McLeod stood and smiled. He walked from the desk and extended his hand to Gray.

"Ay, John Martin Graybeal Graham! I've been expecting you. Let's drag in one of these chairs and we'll have a talk. Thank ye, Eileen."

McLeod was about fifty, had a weathered, but kindly face and a bit of a Scottish burr when he spoke. He was a bit shorter than Gray and somewhat stooped. He had broad shoulders, a muscular upper body and hands that had wielded many picks and shovels.

"Your uncle told me about you," Mac began. "It would appear you have the qualifications to be the principal of our company school. Bill Buck gave me detailed information on your background and experience."

"I'm also working on my masters degree in education," Gray related. "I'm very interested in the principal's position and I can be ready to begin work right away. I understand that one of the first orders of business is to get a new school building constructed."

McLeod nodded.

"Let me give you some background. The county had a school here when we with Selkirk arrived. There were two frame buildings with five rooms in each, but no facilities and no libraries. In one building there was a bookshelf with maybe fifteen or twenty books.

"The state education department closed down the school, but began talking with us about a new facility, knowing that the company couldn't get employees if we didn't have a school. We built the town and a new school, hired and paid the teachers. As things progressed, the county began helping out with the expenses and, in the last few years, have been seeking more control. But Selkirk still is the dominant influence. We still interview and choose the teachers and if something new is needed, we take care of it. We have the funds when the county doesn't.

"How many grades are taught?" Gray asked.

"At present, grades one through eight and we have two years of high school," Mac noted. "We plan to have a full secondary curriculum when we build the new school. We have ten teachers. Most of them are in their twenties and have one or two years of college. We need to have a fully accredited institution for the sons and daughters of all our employees—miners, clerical workers, administrators included."

Gray leaned back and smiled.

"You have a great grasp of education essentials. You also must be a teacher yourself."

"Naw, but I know a wee bit about the learning process," Mac grinned. "I've managed several Selkirk properties and have had some success in building company towns."

"Tell me about your students," Gray asked. "How many do you have?"

"About 500. Most are children of our employees, but we have some from the junction. Our school has a fine reputation and a good number of county residents ask to enroll their youngsters.

"Ay, and our young ones are a fine lot," he smiled. "They're smart and the miners' offspring are rugged due to their lives of hard knocks. And, they're a canny sort."

Gray laughed, recognizing canny as the old country word for careful or clever.

"I'm guessing that you're a native of Scotland."

"Ay, all my McLeods are from the environs of Glasgow. Our lineage has been associated with that area's collieries from long ago. I'm one of the few from my clan, however, to obtain a degree in mining engineering, thanks to a kindly benefactor from Selkirk. After completing my education in Edinburgh, the company asked me to relocate in Pittsburgh and help develop its resources in this country. This is the third operation I've served as a mine supervisor and manager."

Mac swiveled his chair and briefly took a glimpse through the window at the coal tipple.

"I have a love for this work," he said. "It's in my blood. I've dug and loaded coal, graded and shipped it, pulled the injured and dead from disasters and mourned with the families who've lost loved ones. I don't miss a day to go into the mines and spend some time with those who labor there. They're my kinsmen."

Moved by his commentary, Gray saw a softer side of a remarkable man.

"Do you have a family?" he questioned.

"Ay, and that's my second love. I've a wife, two sons and a daughter in Pittsburgh. You've a family as well, I'm told."

"I've a beautiful wife and son who would be eager to accompany me to Citation," Gray replied. "My wife has a teaching certificate also and she could be available to substitute if a faculty member were ill."

"Then we'll have to arrange a place for you and them at our clubhouse."

Gray cocked his head.

"Does that mean I have the job?"

McLeod stood and grasped Gray's hand.

"For one with a name like Graham, how could I say no to a fellow Scotsman?"

CHAPTER FIVE

CONFRONTATION

"Are you Gray Graham?"

The query came from a tall, thin man in a brown suit. He wore a dark brown hat and had a demeanor that provoked confrontation. He was standing just inside the school's front door and was blocking Gray's entry.

"I'm Gray Graham. Who are you?"

"Carson Wells. That name mean anything to you?"

"You're the county judge."

"And not a happy man."

"Is that because of me?"

"You're damn right! You used influence to get the school principal job that was going to my nephew."

Gray felt his temper rising. "You're wrong!" he snapped.

"I don't think so," Wells replied. "You've placed yourself in a bad situation. Your best course is to resign."

Graham shook his head.

"That's not going to happen. And who are you to believe you can tell me what to do?"

"Look, Graham. You have no idea what you're getting into. We've got a powerful political system here and you're not part of it. No outsider can come in and upset the apple cart. I'm warning you. Get out now while you can."

"And, if I don't?"

"You won't like the consequences."

Gray stepped aside and motioned toward the door.

"Take your threat outside, Judge. You've said your piece and we've nothing more to discuss."

Wells glared at Graham then stomped outside.

Gray stood for a moment to regain his composure before walking to his office. Charley Fitzpatrick, a friend and a teacher, was waiting for him.

"I take it you saw Judge Wells," he stated. "I doubt he came to welcome you."

"Just the opposite. He warned me to leave while I could. He threatened retaliation if I didn't. What's this about, Charley?"

Fitzpatrick pulled up a chair and motioned for Gray to join him.

"It's about being top dog," he began. "The real power in this county lies with the school board and the county judge. The board members tell the superintendent what they want and if he doesn't play along they fire him. If a member wants a relative to have a school job he or she will be hired.

"Wells' nephew wanted to be principal of the Citation school and had the backing of his uncle and the school board. But Selkirk mining pays the freight and hires the staff. The county school superintendent had no say.

"I'm certain the board told Liam McCloud who it wanted, but it didn't have the clout to make it happen. And it won't have that authority until and if Citation totally becomes a county school. It's an unusual situation.

"So, the judge and the county school board members are mad as hell. They'll oppose you in any way they can."

"So," Gray remarked, "I should watch my back."

"Exactly," Charley added. "But, remember, you've got the company and all of us at the school behind you. And, I don't think you can be intimidated."

"Where do you think they'll stand where the new school building is concerned?"

"Oh, they'll complain a lot during the construction, but they want it and they'll go along with whatever the company desires," Fitzpatrick said. "After all, the county won't have to pay for it. They may make a token contribution, but they'll be content to let Selkirk Coal bear the cost. All the county wants is control and, eventually, it'll get it."

Construction of the new Citation school building was soon to begin as the November election drew near. But, a formality vote was required to make it acceptable as a county institution. Also, two school board seats were open and Travis Caudill, a U.S. representative, was running for re-election.

Some two weeks before balloting was to take place, an election rally was scheduled at the company theater. It was filled to capacity with miners and other Selkirk employees. They were there in support of Owen Noland, a company foreman, who was running for one of the school board seats.

Judge Wells was chairing the meeting and was on stage with Rep. Caudill, a union representative, Milton Davis—their school board candidate– and several election officials. Graham, Fitzpatrick and other Citation school faculty members were in the audience.

Caudill was vitally interested in what was happening at Citation and was campaigning heavily in the two area precincts. Fitzpatrick nudged Graham as Caudill went on and on about what he had done for Shawnee County.

"Say something, Gray," Charley urged. "We can't let them keep bragging on themselves."

When Caudill paused to take a breath after lauding the school board members and candidate Davis, Graham stood and raised his hand.

"Would the congressman yield the floor?" he asked.

Surprised by the interruption, Caudill reluctantly acquiesced.

"Ladies and gentlemen, I've known Rep. Caudill practically all my life and many of those on the stage for many years," Gray began. "I'm the principal of your school and, as principal, I'm vitally interested in your children as is Owen Noland. We want them to do well, to succeed.

"I want to ask you a question: how often do these men come to see you? You know the answer. They only come at election time. But I'm here throughout the school year as is Owen Noland."

On stage, Caudill and Wells had their heads together, speaking in hushed tones. Graham pivoted and pointed a finger.

"Look at that!" he cried. "They're right now conniving something against your poor little children. I urge you to support our Citation faculty and a man you can trust. Owen, stand up and be recognized!"

Fitzpatrick led the applause as a thundering ovation followed. Wells tried, but failed to halt the demonstration. Reluctantly, he and Caudill led their group to the exit.

"Who in the hell is that man?" Caudill asked.

"A headache we have to eliminate," the judge growled.

But the election would not relieve the pain.

CHAPTER SIX

DISCIPLINE

Judge Wells and the members of the Shawnee County School Board could have bitten a railroad spike in half. They were used to winning but, for the first time, one of their candidates had lost a board seat.

A massive turnout by Selkirk Mining employees and supporters had given Owen Noland a narrow margin of victory over Milton Davis. Wells' henchmen expected approval for the new Citation school building and mistakenly believed that support would carry over into a win for their board candidate.

Wells blamed the loss on School Board Chair Jack Nixon.

"Dammit, Jack!" he screamed. "Who in the hell was that rookie you got as a striker? He was supposed to buy votes, but I bet he kept that money for himself."

"Okay, Carson, we made a mistake," Nixon admitted. "So the vote didn't carry over, so what? We still have a four-to-one board majority so we're still in control. Get over it!"

"Get over it, hell! We've allowed that Selkirk bunch to strengthen its position! That sonuvabitch they hired as principal has rallied their side and who knows what they'll do next. You assured me that my nephew would get that job and told me not to worry nor interfere. But you pussy-footed around and let that asshole McLeod pick somebody else. What are you going to do about that Graham character? He's got to go!"

"I'm working on it!" the board chair barked, "but we can't move too fast. Graham comes from an old school family. His ancestors developed this county and have a lot of respect. His uncle, Bill Buck Graham, is one of the few Republicans to win election in Shawnee, but he got the sheriff's job because of his family ties. You know that and you know that if it hadn't been for Bill Buck, Gray Graham never would have become principal at Citation.

"We can't just run roughshod over him. But, we will move him out. I guarantee it!"

Wells sneered.

"You better be right, Jack, because your future depends on it. I got you elected and re-elected, and I can be your friend or your worst enemy. Don't forget it!"

"Ease up, Carson. This is just a bump in the road."

The next bump would occur at Gray Graham's office.

Gray, fresh from a victory-energized faculty meeting, had just settled in his new office when Pearl Collins knocked on his door.

"Sorry to interrupt, Gray, but I have a group of students here who have asked to see you."

"What's it about?"

"I'm not sure. They just said they have a question they believe is important. Want me to tell them you're busy?"

"No, Pearl, let them in."

Mrs. Collins ushered in six high school students. William Garrett (Little Bull) Elliott appeared to be the group leader. He introduced five others by first name—Roy, Arnold, Jason, Eldon and Jimmy Dan. All were in Gray's classes.

At age fifteen, Little Bull already was man-sized. He stood nearly six-feet tall and weighed a solid 200 pounds. Gray guessed he would outgrow his father, William Hanson (Bull) Elliott, a 6-foot-3, 260-pound giant who had a reputation for his skills handling explosives.

Little Bull came straight to the point.

"Mr. Graham, how do you discipline students you've had trouble with?" he asked.

"Well, I don't know," Gray answered. "I talk to them and find out what the trouble is and…."

"You don't understand," Little Bull interrupted. "We don't like to fool around with things. If we've done something wrong we want to be paddled and get it over with. Do you ever paddle anybody?"

"Well, no, I never have," Gray said.

"Then let me tell you something. You either paddle us or we'll take you out of here."

Gray sat back and narrowed his eyes.

"Wait a minute! You'd better think about that before you ever lay the print of your hand on me! You might not be big enough!"

"Maybe, maybe not," Little Bull responded. "But all six of us are big enough to get it done."

Graham slammed a hand on his desk and stood.

"I'm a fair man, Elliott, but I'll not tolerate insubordination, by you, your companions or anyone else. Any rules we have here will be followed, and anyone who gets out of line will answer to me. I'd rather not discipline by force, but if it becomes necessary, so be it. Do I make myself clear?"

Elliott turned to his companions with question in his eyes. Eldon pursed his lips and nodded his head. No one appeared to disagree. Without another word, they filed out the door.

Gray shook his head and smiled.

'I'd better find my old fraternity paddle,' he thought.

CHAPTER SEVEN

THE THREAT

Not all the students at Citation were sons and daughters of Selkirk employees, such as the ones concerning the paddling issue. The school's reputation was blossoming and youngsters from the junction and other nearby areas were beginning to attend. But additional enrollment also brought additional problems. One morning, two of them stood in the door of Gray Graham's office.

Fred Martin's son, Austin, was a precocious sixth grader. He continually pushed the envelope where his behavior and activities were concerned, so much so, that his teacher, Faith Meriwether, asked that Austin be transferred to a male teacher's classroom. Austin was reassigned to Averill McIntosh's room.

McIntosh was a no-nonsense type. His students towed the line and discovered early on that learning was their only option. Austin did well, but his teacher was cramping his style and his desire for self-expression.

"Mr. Graham, I have a concern," Martin began. "You know my son, Austin, and you also know he can, at times, be a handful. He was reassigned to another classroom recently and Mr. McIntosh is his teacher."

"Mac is tough, but he's a good teacher," Gray said. "How's Austin doing?"

"He's doing okay, but he's scared to death of Mr. McIntosh. He's in constant fear that he's going to be punished and is afraid that his teacher will whip him. I don't think that's healthy."

"I agree," Gray replied. "Mac's a good man and a good teacher, but I don't want any of our students to be afraid of him. Let me make a suggestion. Would it be agreeable if I asked Mac to come to your house and have a conference? If he's okay with that, I think we can clear the air."

"Sounds good," Martin said. "But could Austin still be paddled by Mr. McIntosh?"

"No," Gray stated. "When paddling becomes necessary, I'm the one who'll do it."

Martin's companion, Jim Clayton, interrupted. He had a reputation as a troublemaker.

"Maybe you do too much paddling," he stated. "I understand you laid the wood to nearly thirty students last week for playing on the school steps."

"You heard correctly," Gray acknowledged. "We had a group that ran up and down the outside steps at recess and were concerned that someone was going to get hurt. I told them to stop and, if they didn't, I was going to paddle them.

"One of the girls came up to me last week and said, 'Mr. Graham, they're out there playing on the steps again.' We rounded them up, brought them in and I paddled twenty seven before I stopped. I paddled both boys and girls."

"I hope that tattle-tale was one of them," Clayton cracked.

"She did what she thought was right," Graham related. "Some cried, some said they weren't there, others said they didn't do it. My procedure is to hold their left arm, swat their behind and quit when they bow their back. Usually, only three or four strokes are necessary.

"Do I paddle too much? I do it frequently, but only when it's needed. When a teacher tells me they're having trouble with a child, I say 'send them to me.'"

Clayton cleared his throat and glowered at Graham. He had a distinct dislike for authority figures and was known to have it out with anyone who opposed him.

"I'll tell you one thing, Graham. You sure as hell better never lay a paddle on my son."

"Have I ever paddled your son?" Gray questioned.

"No."

"Is he due for a paddling?"

"No, and I'm warning you. You're not going to paddle any child of mine."

Gray reached behind and took his "persuader" from the windowsill.

"This is the paddle I use right here," he stated. "If I ever have to paddle your son, this is what I'll use. And, you can be certain, he'll be treated just like everybody else."

With that, Gray slammed the paddle against the desktop. The sound was like that of a pistol shot, but it emphasized his point. He was in charge and also could be trouble.

Clayton stood abruptly, upturning his chair.

"You whip my son and I'll whip you!" he declared.

"You might be able to do that, but I won't be standing by twiddling my thumbs," Gray retorted. "And, you can be sure I'll get a big piece out of your hide.

"Anytime you want to take me on, you know where to find me. School's out at 3:30 and you can meet me at the railroad tracks a few minutes later. I walk the tracks back to the clubhouse about 3:45."

Clayton slammed a fist against the palm of his other hand.

"I've changed my mind, Graham. You don't have to whip my son for me to clean your plow. I'll do it when you least expect it."

"Meaning what?"

"Meaning one day you'll walk the tracks when your guard's down. That's when I'll be there."

Charley Fitzpatrick appeared as Martin and Clayton departed.

"Damn, Gray, do you have a death wish? That Clayton fellow is bad news. He holds a grudge like you wouldn't believe. I heard the tail end of your conversation in the hall and he doesn't make idle threats. You'd better carry some protection."

"What are you suggesting?" Gray asked.

"I've got a snub-nosed .38 in my car. It's yours for the asking. Stick it in your waistband and keep it handy when you're alone."

"Sorry, Charley, I'm not looking to get into a shooting match."

"Look, Gray, I'm not talking about a shootout, I'm talking about protecting yourself. If I were in your place, I'd kill Jim Clayton before I'd ever let him whip me."

"I don't think he can whip me."

"Maybe not, but he could put a big hurt on you and you can't afford to take that chance. Meet me down at the tracks after school. I drove in today and I've got the pistol stashed under the front seat."

Charley left before Gray could further resist.

Although he tried to avoid him, Gray found Charley waiting near the tracks. A flannel sack was thrust into Graham's coat pocket.

"The pistol isn't loaded, but I've got a box of shells with the weapon," Charley said. "Keep one chamber open for safety. You don't want it going off by accident."

CHAPTER EIGHT

WARNING

Gray stowed the revolver in a back corner of a closet shelf. He knew how to use the weapon, but despite the persuasion of Charley Fitzpatrick, he was reluctant to carry it. His quick temper could fuel the impetus to use it.

Charley's warnings, however, were not to be discarded. The Judge and the school board could be formidable opponents, and hotheads like Jim Clayton could create immediate difficulties. And, more trouble was just around the corner.

Jack Nixon had an unlimited number of financial resources. His funds came from wildcat mines, moonshining and many other illegal endeavors. But his real moneymaker came in the form of bootleg coal.

Early in thirty-one, Nixon offered out-of-work coal miners jobs digging out coal from atop underground mines. Using picks and shovels, they loaded the mineral into sacks, placed it in small trucks they rented from Nixon, who sold the "black gold" from one to three dollars cheaper than regularly mined coal.

Most of the stolen coal was taken from areas the company never would touch as it was not economical for them to mine it. Shafts just big enough for a single individual would be dug as deep as necessary. Sometimes those shafts required the use of lamps, hoisting ropes and dynamite, all items that Nixon would provide, again for a price.

He established and expanded bootleg mining throughout Southeastern Kentucky, and made out like the successful bandit he was. Money meant power, especially during the height of the nation's economic depression. In his home county of Shawnee, Nixon used the school board as his power base, a brotherhood in which he sparkled and in which he delighted. He wasn't about to allow a lowly school principal to mess it up. He wrestled with solutions and, finally, came up with a plausible plan. The board chairman was in a good mood as he arrived at Wells' office.

"You're going to like this," Jack began. "I've come up with a way to get rid of Gray Graham. It has several options. And, if one plan doesn't work, the other one will."

Wells gave Nixon a skeptical look.

"Okay, let's hear it."

"First of all, it's not advisable to use bodily harm, at least not at this point. If we were to take out Graham right now, the initial suspects would be the school board members or maybe you or me. And his uncle, the sheriff, would be after the incident like ugly on an ape.

"Now, it's common knowledge that Graham has stepped on some toes and made a few enemies. One of those enemies is Jim Clayton. I understand he and Clayton got into a shouting match and Clayton has vowed to 'clean his plow.' It had something to do about paddling a student, but, nevertheless, it was a threat."

"Clayton is a problem just waiting to happen," Wells stated. "Everybody knows that. He's always popping off about one thing or another."

"That's a fact!" Nixon agreed. "He has a bad temper and when it boils over he goes to war. Think about how many times he's been arrested for fighting. How often have you heard it said that 'one of these days, he's going to kill somebody?'"

"Go on," Wells prompted.

"Well, let's set the stage for something like that to happen. We've got a policeman over at Brushy Fork Mining who's done some 'light work' for us. He's one helluva marksman and we've used him on occasion to put the fear of God into some people who've given us problems. Graham walks the tracks back to the Selkirk clubhouse at the end of the school day. Our man can be situated on the side of the mountain to take a few shots at Graham. Not to injure, but enough near hits to make him take cover. We do this several times, letting him know that he has a serious enemy.

"Graham won't scare easily, but those warning shots will give him pause. We'll also get the word around that Jim Clayton has threatened him and may be behind the shooting."

Wells scoffed at the scheme.

"Clayton won't go after anyone with a rifle," he said. "He'll either provoke a fistfight or go for a pistol."

"But, hear me out!" Nixon continued. "If we can't scare off Graham, we go to the second option. Our policeman also is good with a handgun. If he shoots Graham with a pistol and makes it appear as a confrontation with Clayton, we've solved our problem."

Wells stroked his chin and paused in thought.

"It might work," he said. "Who's our man with the gun?"

"That fellow from Detroit we hired as a marshal when we had that Brushy Fork disturbance. He's Italian, believe his name is Rossi."

Wells recognized the name.

"Yeah, he was the mob hit man. Had to get out of town in a hurry. He's smooth and good-looking, just the ticket we need.

"Get him over here and put things in motion. If we do this right, we could solve this problem in a hurry. What about Bill Buck Graham?"

"If we have to kill Graham, everything should point to Jim Clayton as the murder suspect and we may have to take some extra steps to make him appear guilty," Jack said. "If we were to plant a pistol on him—the murder weapon—Bill Buck could be convinced he had the right man.

"The most popular weapon in the coal fields is a Smith and Wesson .38. Rossi could do the job with such a pistol and plant it in Clayton's possession. The murder weapon could be used, or another could be substituted as long as the empty rounds matched those used to kill Graham."

"What about fingerprints? Would we have a problem with the FBI?"

"Probably not. The Feds got into fingerprint cards about ten years ago, but we're considered too backwoodsy to be included. To be on the safe side, the weapon would have to be wiped clean or Clayton's prints would have to be on it. It'd be easier to substitute a clean pistol. In fact, our enforcer probably would prefer it."

"Why's that?" Wells asked.

"These mob men are a funny breed," Nixon stated. "They get comfortable with certain weapons and are hesitant to give them up."

Wells drummed his fingers on the desk.

"Tell me again. What's this Dago's name?"

"Rossi, Vito Rossi."

"Bring him in. Let's have a talk with Vito."

CHAPTER NINE

DEALING

Jim Clayton was the least of Gray Graham's worries. An immediate concern was the school library. Citation School had a few reference books, but was many dollars short in its ability to fund a library. Graham sought to remedy that by promoting school plays, bake sales and any other activity that would yield a few dollars. It was a tough task during the height of the Depression.

Bernice Burden, a senior member of the faculty, was the unofficial treasurer for the project. She kept the money in a padlocked box and stashed it in a locked desk drawer, reflecting her continuing distrust of banks. Unfortunately, rudimentary banking systems can easily be broken.

Gray had just entered his office Monday morning when Bernice arrived.

"Something awful has happened!" she began. "We've lost all our library money!"

A shocked principal was unable to comment before Bernice continued.

"I took the box with our library money home Friday after school and put it in a bureau drawer after making an accounting," she said. "I was going to bring it back to school this morning, but found the lock broken and all the cash missing."

"Someone stole it!" Gray exclaimed. "But who?"

"I'm sorry to say that Fred did."

Fred Burden, Bernice's husband, was a miner who loved to drink and gamble and seldom had funds of his own. It was said that money passed through his hands "like slippery on an eel." His life was filled with contrasts and, in short, he was an enigma.

Burden was bright, had graduated from high school and was a good halfback on the football team. Academics bored him, and he was more interested in having a good time than pursuing a career. No one understood why he'd settled for work in the coal mines. The couple lived on Bernice's meager salary.

Gray, who had never met Burden, was surprised to learn that of all people, Bernice's husband had absconded with the funds. He listened as she continued.

"I confronted Fred," she said, "and he finally admitted that he'd taken the money and lost it playing pool down at Cornette's."

Cornette's was a liquor and pool hall located in the junction. Many a paycheck was squandered there, a haven for pool and card sharks.

"What can I say?" Bernice tearfully questioned. "I don't want Fred arrested and it wouldn't do any good if he were jailed. That won't get our money back. I can't begin to tell you how sorry I am. What can I do to make this right?"

"How much was in the till?" Gray asked.

"A little more than $500," she replied.

"Do you know how he lost it?"

"He was playing eight ball against one of Cornette's best—Everett Wesley."

"I know the name," Gray stated. "Isn't he the one who looks like some cowboy movie actor?"

"William S. Hart," Bernice said.

"Yeah, he was a big star before the talkies came in," Gray smiled. "Hart was one of my heroes. He was the noble cowboy, tough, honest, loyal and always fair.

"So, Hart has a look-alike in Wesley. I wonder if he has Hart's fairness trait?"

"What do you mean?" Bernice asked.

"Well, it won't hurt if I paid a visit to Mr. Wesley. If he plays fair, maybe we can get our money back."

Gray drove over to Cornette's after school and had no trouble identifying Everett Wesley. Tall and rugged looking, Wesley stood at the bar, a pool cue in one hand and a beer in the other. He was a mirror image of William S. Hart. With a ten-gallon hat and a six-shooter, he easily could double for the Western star.

Ordering a beer, Gray stood next to Wesley, who had his back to him as he talked with a companion. His friend left and Wesley faced the barkeep, motioning for another brew.

"Ever see the movie *Tumbleweeds*?" Gray asked, staring straight ahead.

The startled Wesley turned his head toward Graham.

"What'd you say?"

"Ever see the movie *Tumbleweeds*?"

Wesley studied his questioner for a moment before answering.

"Yeah, I've seen it. What about it?"

"It starred one of my favorite cowboy actors, William S. Hart," Gray related.

"So, what's your point?"

"Hart was sort of a role model for all of us youngsters back in the twenties," Gray continued. "He was tough, could be mean as hell, but was always fair and honest. Good character traits."

Wesley took a swallow from his bottle.

"I agree."

"You could be Hart's twin brother," Graham continued.

"So I'm told."

Gray turned to face Wesley.

"You look like him, but I wonder if you can act like him?"

"Not me, friend," Wesley commented. "I'm no movie star."

"I don't mean act in that way." Graham said. "I mean respond to people in a fair and honest way."

Wesley frowned and placed a hand on the bar.

"What are you getting at? And, who in the hell are you anyway?"

"I'm Gray Graham, principal of the Selkirk Mining school at Citation. The husband of one of my teachers lost $500 to you playing eight ball. The money wasn't his. It was school money being saved to start a library. Without that money we're up the creek. No money, no library."

"Too bad, schoolman. I feel sorry for you and the school," Wesley lamented.

"Thought you might like to help us?" Gray remarked. "Sort of give the money back as a contribution. That's something William S. Hart would do."

Wesley appeared bewildered, then began to laugh.

"I may look like Hart, but I'm not a bleeding heart. I'm a pool player, a gambler, I make my living winning games of chance. I don't eat if I don't win. And, I like to eat."

"It doesn't bother you that you're short-changing some fine young people?" Gray questioned.

"That's not my problem. Your friend chose to play and, hopefully, win some of my money. He took a chance and it didn't happen. He's the one to blame. I can't help you, schoolman."

Gray took a pool cue and rolled it against a table's felt top. Wesley took notice.

"Do you play?"

"Yeah."

"Are you any good? Think you could beat me?"

Graham shrugged and smiled.

"Tell you what," Wesley offered. "Let's play some eight ball. You win and you'll get back the money for your library. I'll play you for ten dollars a game."

"I'm a school teacher," Gray said. "I don't have that kind of money."

Proprietor Cameron Cornette interceded.

"My son goes to your school," he said. "I know Liam McLeod and he was kind enough to let me enroll him at Citation."

"Is Leonard Cornette your boy?" Graham queried. "He's a fine young man."

"Ev, I'd like to see this man play you," Cornette said. "I'm willing to back him and find out if he's as good a pool player as he is a school man. What do you say?"

Before Wesley could answer, Cam turned to Graham.

"Is this okay with you."

Wesley's response covered it.

"Let's play pool," he said.

CHAPTER TEN

THE GAME

Gray swept his hand across the table's playing surface.

"Is this the high stakes table?" he grinned.

"It could be," Wesley offered. "Tell you what. No need to lag for break. Let's see what you've got. Rack 'em, Cam."

Graham took his position at the right end of the table and lined up the cue ball. He sighted his stick for the fourth ball on the right and followed through with a smooth, but powerful stroke.

The Galaxy break pocketed three balls and opened a nice spread of comfortable shots.

"Three ball in the corner pocket," Gray called. He stroked the cue ball below center, sank the three and back-spun the white rock. He continued to play position and ran the table with ease.

"He's got a dead stroke," Cornette whispered to Wesley, indicating that Graham played flawlessly.

Ev nodded in agreement.

"But, can he keep it up?" he questioned.

After five games, Wesley was up one game. In game six, Graham had the eight ball frozen against the rail and faced a head-on shot.

"I like this guy," Cam murmured, "but the pressure's on. I don't think he can make it."

Ev rolled his tongue against a cheek.

"Ten bucks says he makes it."

"You're on," Cornette said.

The shot was from a distance and required the right touch and correct English. Gray studied for a moment and lined it up with confidence.

He smoothly stroked the cue ball, giving it a left spin. It touched the cushion, spun properly and the eight ball rolled cleanly into the pocket.

"That makes us even," Wesley noted. "Let's take a break and get a beer."

Cornette walked ahead and got three bottles.

"Mind if I join you?" he asked.

"How can I say no to my bankroller?" Graham grinned.

Gray turned to his opponent.

"How long have you been a pool hustler?" he asked.

"Didn't think you'd notice," Ev deadpanned. "Think I'm hustling you?"

"I'm not sure as yet. Do you have another occupation?"

Wesley placed his bottle on the bar and sighed.

"It's a long story," he said.

"I'm a good listener."

Cornette opened more bottles and nodded at Wesley.

"Tell him, Ev," he encouraged.

Wesley grasped the new brew, backed against the bar and placed his elbows on its surface.

"I'm a drunkard, schoolman," he began. "I'm from upstate New York and have a college degree in mining engineering. I got married, had a son and was doing well until my wife met another man she liked better than me. She left when I was at work, took the boy and I never heard from either of them again. I tried to find them, but had no luck. It was just like they were swallowed up and the world refused to spit them out.

"I hit the bottle pretty hard and drifted from job to job, losing good employment because of my drinking. I passed out in some backwater town and found myself on a southbound train one night not knowing where it was headed. I ended up in the Kentucky-West Virginia coalfields, but it was the same old story. I'd get a decent job, but couldn't quit drinking and the job would disappear. I ended up here and Cam took me in and has tried to get me sober. All I've accomplished is to substitute beer for the whiskey, but Cornette lets me sleep in back and run the pool hall."

Ev shook his head and chuckled.

"You asked me if I'd ever seen *Tumbleweeds.*"

"Did you like it?" Gray asked.

"Like it? Hell, I was in it!"

A surprised Graham asked him to continue.

"When I was in New York, I met Bill Hart. He's a native of Newburgh, an old Hudson River town north of New York City. He was amazed at how much we looked alike and asked me to accompany him to Hollywood. He said he'd see that I was hired on as his movie double. *Tumbleweeds* was going to be his comeback picture. This was in twenty-five when Tom Mix became popular and Bill and Hoot Gibson saw their cowboy careers decline.

"I couldn't ride a horse, but I could fight like hell and did several scenes as Bill's extra. Unfortunately, I didn't fake-fight very well and knocked out another actor and injured several others. I was fired and took the train back to New York to find that my wife had left me.

"I saw *Tumbleweeds* in a theater and recognized myself in several scenes. The film was only a minor success and I never saw Bill again. He was quite a guy, not unlike the straight shooters he played in his films."

Gray slapped Wesley's shoulder.

"I never thought I'd be playing pool against a movie star."

"You're not," Ev grimaced. "Just a worn-out old timer who doesn't even hustle pool very well. Get your stick and let's finish this."

He motioned to Cornette.

"Will you back my friend here in a final winner-take-all?"

Cam wiped the bar and glanced at Gray.

"I'm game if you are?"

Graham dribbled the butt of his cue on the floor before responding.

"Let's get this straight. If I win, Wesley gives me $500. But, what if I lose?"

Cornette shrugged his shoulders.

"Then I pay off Ev, here. You're not beholden to me, won't owe me anything. But, honestly, I think you can beat him. How about it?"

Cocking his head, Gray moved to the table.

"Let's play pool," he said.

Both played well, but performed so well defensively that neither had a decent shot. Finally, only three balls remained—a stripe, a solid and the eight ball. Gray, playing stripes, had a straight shot for the top left corner pocket and chose for a draw shot on the ten to bring the cue ball back to the center table.

That, he reasoned, would give him good position to go for the eight in the side pocket and the win. But, he missed. The ten rattled in the pocket and came out. The cue ball did come back to center table, but

Wesley had a difficult shot. His solid, the five, was nearly against the eight. His only alternative was to go off center on the ball, bank it off the top rail and hope to sink it in the right corner pocket.

Wesley studied his possibilities and eyed his shot carefully. What was he doing, Graham pondered? Ev had no chance of pocketing the ball unless he cut it just right.

Moving his hand toward the end of the stick and creating a short bridge with his left hand, Wesley made his shot quick and hard. The five banged against the top cushion, angled into the right corner pocket and the eight ball nestled in the side pocket. Graham stared in disbelief.

"How did you do that?" he asked.

"With a little skill and a lot of luck," Wesley declared. "Sorry, schoolman, you lose."

CHAPTER ELEVEN

FIRST SHOT

Gray was determined to overcome his pool hall defeat. But he wasn't out of the woods yet where adversity was concerned. Another issue lay ahead as he trudged down the railroad tracks.

His initial reaction was surprise as the gravel in his path exploded across his shoes. It happened again as he prepared to resume his walk.

When his hat was jerked from his head, Graham realized he was someone's shooting target and sought cover by sliding down the railroad embankment. He had heard no sound, no report from a weapon, but the hole in his hat was evidence of an assassination attempt.

Gray slid farther down the embankment, seeking more cover. He lay still, anticipating more from the shooter. Minutes that seemed like hours passed, but no more shots were fired. Looking to his left, he saw his hat and stretched to reach it. Grasping its brim, he spun the headpiece up and onto the tracks. There was no reaction.

Charley Fitzpatrick was delayed and didn't leave the schoolhouse until Gray had departed. He, too, was walking the tracks some fifteen minutes later and spied the hat.

"Get down, Charley!"

Fitzpatrick heard the voice, but couldn't locate the speaker.

"Dammit, Charley, get down! Somebody's shooting at me!"

Puzzled, Fitzpatrick stooped to retrieve the hat. It was jerked from his hands by a silent force. The schoolteacher twisted to follow its flight and saw Graham at the base of the shallow embankment. He acknowledged the hand motion to join him, diving headfirst and rolling to a stop beside Graham.

"What the hell's going on?"

"Don't know, Charley. Someone's up on the hill and has been shooting at me. I'm guessing he has a rifle with a silencer. I can't see anyone and he's too far away to be using a handgun."

"Have you been hit?"

"No, and I don't know why. I couldn't have been a better target. He's either a lousy shot or just trying the scare the hell out of me."

Charley peered at the hillside, seeing no trace of an assailant.

"Are you scared?"

"No, I'm having the time of my life! Hell yes I'm scared!"

Fitzpatrick again scanned the hillside.

"Do you have that gun I gave you?"

Graham refused to look at him. After a long pause, he responded.

"It's at home," he said.

Charley shook his head in disgust.

"You knucklehead! You didn't listen to anything I said! I warned you this could happen! If you had that pistol we could shoot our way out of this."

"And just how could we do that, Charley?" Gray sneered. "We can't even see who's doing the shooting and he's too far away for a pistol to be of any use!"

Fitzpatrick rolled onto his back and licked his lips. His mind was racing as he sought a solution.

"Wait!" he cried. "Maybe a train will come by. We could jump it or escape by running alongside it."

"Come on, Charley!" Gray growled. "It's going on toward five o'clock. No train is due here until tomorrow morning."

Graham followed his companion's example and rolled onto his back. Each stared into space, lost in thought.

"Wonder who's shooting at us?" Charley pondered. "Bet it's Jim Clayton. He's already threatened you and he's just mean enough to take a shot. Now, if you'd just kept that .38 handy...."

"Forget it, Charley! We've already covered that. Besides, Clayton wouldn't use a rifle, he'd like to be close up with a pistol. Anyway, I think he's all talk. I've given him plenty of time to do something and I can't believe he's waited all these weeks to do this."

"Who else is upset with you?" Fitzpatrick asked, then added. "Forget I said that. You've made more people mad in a few months than I have in a lifetime. You're going to make Selkirk believe it's hired the wrong principal."

Gray spat in displeasure.

"Thanks a lot, Charley! I appreciate your continued support!"

"I didn't mean it that way," Fitzpatrick apologized. "You've done a lot of good things, but stepped on some toes doing it. Judge Wells' nephew is a loser, he never could have made a good principal."

Neither commented during the next few minutes. Suddenly, Charley sat up straight.

"That's it, Gray! Judge Wells!"

Gray grabbed Charley's coat and dragged him down.

"You idiot! Are you trying to get yourself killed?"

Fitzpatrick pushed Graham away and resumed his back-to-the gravel position.

"Think about it, Gray? Who's been more upset with you than the Judge? He ordered you to get out of town or suffer the consequences. Then, you were a key in getting Owen Noland elected to the school board. That's on top of Wells' nephew losing out as principal. All of a sudden, his political hold on Shawnee County is under siege. He needs you gone."

Graham considered Fitzpatrick's comments.

"You could be right, Charley, but I don't think that's the judge up there with a weapon on us."

"Of course not, but it's probably one of the judge's cohorts. And don't forget Jack Nixon. He's as mean as a striped snake and he and the Judge have controlled this county for years. Nixon controls the school board with an iron hand while his other hand is in any illegal enterprise you could imagine. If anyone could find and hire a hit man, Nixon could."

"Makes sense, Charley," Gray agreed, "but killing me is going to the extreme. It could raise a lot of questions, and the Judge would rather get rid of me in a more logical manner."

Fitzpatrick edged up the embankment and squinted across the rails.

"I wonder if our friend is still there?" he whispered. "We haven't heard from him in a while."

"Well, there's one way to find out," Graham suggested. "We've thought of everything else, maybe we should just make a run for it."

"I don't know," Charley reflected. "We'd be taking a big chance."

"Think about it, Charley. We'll have to run fast and it's hard to hit a moving target."

"Yeah, but I'm wearing a new pair of shoes. I don't know if I can run very well."

"Forget it, Charley," Gray laughed, pulling Fitzpatrick to his feet. "We'll probably get killed anyway."

CHAPTER TWELVE

FAIR AND HONEST

"I'm supposed to give this to you."

Leonard Cornette handed Gray a soiled sealed envelope as the social studies class ended. Leonard began shaking his head side-to-side as his teacher prepared to speak.

"Don't ask, Mr. Graham. All I know is that my dad told me to give this to you. I don't know anything else about it."

Gray gently shook the envelope.

"I guess it isn't loaded," he smiled.

Leonard shrugged his shoulders and walked out the door. He'd completed his task, but wasn't happy about it.

Gray tore open the envelope and removed the folded message. It was written in a clear and neat cursive style.

Mr. Graham –
I need to talk with you. Please see me at Cornette's.
Everett Wesley

Wesley was playing pool when Gray arrived at Cornette's. Cam Cornette caught his eye and waved Graham over to the bar. He opened a bottle of beer and sat in before his visitor.

"Thanks, Cam, but I'll take a rain check," Gray said.

"Drink up, it's on the house," the barkeep replied. "You may need to fortify yourself before talking with Everett. I assume you're here because of his note."

"Have you read it?"

"No, Wesley gave it to me and asked if I could have it delivered to you at the school. I handed the note to Leonard and told him to make sure you got it."

"And, he didn't seem too happy about it," Gray noted.

"Leonard doesn't like Everett. He thinks he's a cheat and a low-life."

Cam wiped down the bar top and responded to Gray's questioning look.

"Early on, Leonard used to rack for Ev, but got disgusted with the way he hustled everyone. He wants nothing to do with him and I had to force him to deliver that note. He probably thinks he hustled you."

"He's pretty opinionated for a young teenager," Graham observed.

"In case you didn't know, those kids at Citation respect you. They like upright people," Cam called over his shoulder as he stepped toward another customer.

Gray leaned against the bar, watching Wesley run the table against his latest victim. His disgusted opponent threw some bills on the table followed by his stick. Ev scooped up his winnings and, not seeing another candidate, joined Graham. He motioned to Cam with two fingers and guided Gray to a pool table in the corner.

"What did you think of my winning shot?" Wesley asked, referring to their deciding round of eight ball.

"I don't think you could make that shot again," Gray declared.

"Let's see," Everett proposed.

He searched the pockets for the five and eight ball. He placed them in the same position as before and located the cue ball nearby.

"You try it first," he ordered. "Believe the five was a solid."

Taking his time, Gray sought the proper angle for a five-eight combination. His stroke was smooth and he made the five, but the eight remained.

"That's one of the best bank shots I've ever made!" he exclaimed.

"But, you didn't make the eight ball," Wesley emphasized.

"And, as I said, I don't think you can make that combination again," Gray repeated.

Wesley lined up the balls and took his stance.

"As I said, this shot requires a little skill and a lot of luck."

With a long stick and short bridge, Ev power-stroked the cue ball. This time, the five rattled in the corner pocket, but fell. The eight-ball dropped immediately in the side pocket.

"Okay, how did you do it?" Graham demanded.

"Simple, I cheated. It's a hustle shot. I have to hit the object ball just right to make it. But, I follow through and hit the eight ball directly into the side pocket. I have to do it so quickly that the illegal hit on the eight goes unnoticed."

"Why are you telling me this?"

"Because, dammit, you got to me! It was all that talk about Bill Hart portraying a fair and honest cowboy. Bill wasn't just playing a role, he really was a fair and honest man. I look like him, I doubled for him and, on film, I would appear to be just as fair and honest as he was.

"I made the mistake of thinking too much and became ashamed of myself."

Wesley took a long pull from his beer and stared at the floor.

"I can spot a sucker as soon as he walks in the door. Fred Burden came in here all liquored-up and spoiling for a fight. He peeled off a bill from a good-sized roll, bought a beer and started eyeing me. He was a chicken just waiting to be plucked.

"I threw out balls on the table, not caring where they went and taking random shots. He kept staring and I knew I had him.

"'Who wants to fight?' he hollered. "Everyone ignored him, but he kept it up and said he could whip anyone in the place. I said I wouldn't fight him, but I'd play him a game of pool, emphasizing that he might add to his bankroll.

"I did the usual, losing the first few games, buying the beer and letting him think he had the upper hand. Then, I started winning a few and we'd go back and forth that way until I suggested we get serious and raise the stakes. If the mark believes he can take you, and Fred was drunk enough to think so, he'll take the bait.

"That's when I took him. I told him I'd never been so lucky and just hoped my luck wouldn't run out. Fred kept playing and insisted my winning streak was a fluke. By now, he was losing consistently and finally said he'd had enough.

"I told him I really was sorry he was losing so much money, but suggested we play double or nothing so he could recoup some of his losses. I talked him into it and cleaned him out."

Wesley finished his beer and reached into a pocket.

"Here," he said. "Take this."

Gray was handed a roll of bills.

"There's $500 there, plus some money won off side bets."

"What's the catch?" Graham asked.

"No catch. Just take it and buy your books."

Gray stuffed the bills into a pocket and took a long look at Wesley.

"Why don't you really get on the wagon, Everett? I bet you were quite a man once and, if you sober up, you can be that person again. I bet you could make Bill Hart proud."

Wesley chuckled.

"You're a dreamer, schoolman, and you gave me a guilty conscience. But life isn't like *Tumbleweeds*."

Ev turned and addressed the crowd.

"Anybody up for a game of pool?"

CHAPTER THIRTEEN

NECESSITIES

With the library funds restored and a refurbished peace of mind, Graham strode into the classroom and glanced again at his lesson plan. He scanned the room and saw Jimmy Dan Trivette staring out the window.

Jimmy Dan was the dumbest kid in school. That's what he said and all his classmates agreed. But the youngster had a winning personality and was well liked.

Gray had Jimmy Dan, or J.D. as his male friends called him, in several classes. Most of the muscular youngster's teachers had given up on him academically, but Graham saw him as a challenge.

J.D. had little or no interest in his classes and spent most of his time staring out the window. Gray, frustrated by the time he'd had to spend fighting political fires, dodging bullets and recouping the stolen library funds, was eager to focus on teaching. And, Jimmy Dan was his target.

Today's social studies lesson concerned the basics of life and Gray directed many of his questions at his reluctant student. Jimmy Dan's pat answer was "I don't know," repeated so many times that it became embarrassing.

"Mr. Graham, don't call on me anymore," he demanded.

"Why not?" the teacher asked.

"Because I'm dumb," J.D. said. "Everybody knows that. I don't know anything."

When the class's smiles and laughter subsided, Gray sat on the edge of his desk, folded his arms and stared at the youngster for a moment.

"You're not dumb, J.D. Everybody knows something and everyone can learn."

Jimmy Dan shook his head.

"Not me," he said.

"Do you know where you live?" Gray asked.

"Sure," J.D. replied

"Do you know how to eat and how to dress yourself?"

Little Bull couldn't contain himself.

"Take your time, J.D.," he laughed.

Gray spun around and pointed at the speaker.

"That's enough, Elliott!" he snapped.

"Okay, J.D., answer my question. Do you know how to eat and how to dress yourself?"

"Sure, Mr. Graham. Everybody knows how to do that."

Lisa Wallace raised her hand.

"But, Mr. Graham, aren't those things just a reflex—a reaction or a biological response?"

The teacher nodded in agreement.

"Eating is because it's associated with one of the necessities of life. And, so is being able to clothe yourself. But you don't always wear the same clothing, you have to learn how to put on different things."

"And, so," he said, turning back to Jimmy Dan, "this is something you had to learn."

J.D.'s blank stare turned to recognition.

"Yeah, I guess that's right," he said.

"So, that shows you can learn," Gray explained.

"You said something about the necessities of life," Lisa commented. "What do you mean?"

"Well, basically, there are three necessities of life—food, clothing and shelter," Graham said. "We have to have those things to survive. And, if we don't survive, nothing else makes any difference. This is why they're basic necessities. They provide our foundation, our base for doing other things in life."

"How do we get them?" Jimmy Dan asked.

"Think about it, J.D. Where do we get food?"

"Well, from the company store or a grocery store."

"And, where do those places get it."

James Harrison raised his hand. He was one of the students whose family lived in the county. His father had died some time ago.

"They get some of it from my grandfather Harrison's farm," he announced.

"What animals does your granddad have on that farm?" the teacher asked. "Does he have any sheep?"

"Yeah, he has a few along with some beef cattle. He slaughters and sells some for food, but Papaw also shears the sheep and sells the wool."

"And," Gray turned to Jimmy Dan, "we eat that food from Mr. Harrison's farm that's sold in the grocery store as beef and mutton. But what happens to that wool, how's it used?"

Jimmy Dan shook his head.

"I don't know," he said.

Gray stood and pointed to the back of J.D.'s chair.

"Is that your jacket hanging there?"

"Yeah."

"What kind of material is it made from?" Gray asked.

Jimmy Dan fingered the red and black fabric.

"It feels like wool," he said.

"And where do we get wool?"

"From granddad Harrison's farm?" he hesitantly responded.

The class laughed and Graham slapped on his desk for silence.

"Of course from the Harrison farm and others where sheep are raised and sheared. And, the wool that's sheared is made into clothing, just like your jacket," he said, pointing to Jimmy Dan.

Surveying the students, Gray singled out Ralph Johnson.

"What line of work is your father in?" he asked.

"He's a builder, a contractor for the mining company"

"Does he build houses?" Gray asked.

"Well, sure," Ralph acknowledged. "We came down here from Pittsburgh so my dad could build houses for Citation."

"Did you know that, J.D.?"

Jimmy Dan nodded that he did.

"And, what are those houses used for?" Gray questioned. "In which of the necessities of life does housing fit? I'm asking you, J.D."

The student looked like a deer caught in the headlights.

"Well…" he began hesitantly.

"Think about it, J.D. We've said that food and clothing come from the Harrison family farm. What's the one category we have left?"

"Shelter?" Jimmy Dan asked with a nervous smile.

"You've got it!" Gray exclaimed, walking to the chalkboard. "You're using your head!"

Quickly, he wrote "The Necessities of Life" and under that heading he listed "Food, Clothing, Shelter."

"J.D.! Copy that down in your notebook and, when you've done it, tell me what you've written."

The class watched Graham as they waited for J.D. to finish. When Jimmy Dan looked up, the teacher pointed to him and asked to hear what he'd written. J.D. responded and did so with a smile.

"Now listen closely, J.D." Gray stated. "I'm going to ask you at least once every day what the three necessities of life are. And, you're going to tell me. Got it?"

"Yessir," the student grinned.

"Yes sir what?"

"Uh, yes sir, food, clothing and shelter."

Graham tossed his textbook on a table. He sat on the edge of his desk and spoke about an upcoming exam and continued talking with his students rather than lecturing.

Suddenly, Gray spun to his right and pointed to Jimmy Dan.

"What are the necessities of life?"

J.D.'s eyes widened in shock before recollection surfaced.

"Food, clothing and shelter!" he shouted.

"Way to go!" the teacher acknowledged. "Who says you can't learn!"

Mary Montgomery raised her hand.

"Remember earlier when we were talking about the Necessities of Life? You said that James' family raised sheep that provided food and clothing. And, that Ralph's father built houses for shelter. But, how do other jobs fit in? Lisa's father is the town doctor. Don't doctors provide a necessity of life?"

"Good point, Mary. What do you think, Lisa?"

"Hey, I agree," she said. "My father makes sick people well and, without doctors, we wouldn't be healthy. And besides, I have food, clothing and shelter because of what my daddy does."

"So do I," James said. "And, don't forget, my granddad not only provides for my family, but provides two of the necessities of life for all of us."

Others began to chime in.

"My father's a dentist at the junction. Isn't that a necessity?"

"My dad's a great mechanic. He can fix anything. If something breaks down in the mines, he'll fix it. Now that's a real necessity."

The contributions went on and on, from occupation to occupation and beyond.

Finally, Gray halted all the talk.

"You've made some good points and have raised some interesting questions. Now, does anybody have some answers? What does all this mean?"

Some mumbled and others shook their heads.

"J.D.," Graham called. "We've heard from everyone but you. Any thoughts?"

"Gosh, Mr. Graham, what do I know? I've told you how dumb…"

"Stop it!" the teacher cried. "You've already shown that you can learn. Now, think about what you've learned and what you've heard today. Does any of this make sense? We all have families with different jobs, how does this fit in with the Necessities of Life?"

Everyone looked at J.D., who gazed out the window. Gray held up his hand for silence and they all waited.

"J.D.?" Graham questioned.

"My daddy was hurt in the mines and doesn't have steady work," the youngster finally began. "He just finds work when he can. My mother takes in washing and what she does gives us food, clothing and shelter. And, my brothers and sisters and I do what we can to help out. And, I guess that's enough to get by.

"Mom says she wishes she and Dad hadn't dropped out of school. That's kept them from having good jobs. And that's why she won't let me quit school. I've told her I can't learn, but she says I'll never learn if I drop out."

Jimmy Dan looked down, obviously embarrassed. He swallowed and looked up at the class.

"All of you are smart and can learn," he said. "And your moms and dads are smart and have steady jobs. I listened to all that you said and I know that you're going to have good lives and do good things."

J.D. turned and looked directly at his teacher.

"I believe you, Mr. Graham. You did something good when you made me learn about the Necessities of Life. And when I heard Lisa, James and Ralph—and all the others—talk about their families and what they did, I know that all of them are important.

"We have to have food, clothing and shelter," he continued. "But doctors and people who can fix things do important and necessary things, too.

I guess we have to have all these people to have the important things. It makes sense that we first have to have the necessities of life before we can make things better, have good jobs, and do good things.

"My mom says it's also important for our family to work together. That's a good thing, too. It's kind of like playing baseball. You have to get to first base before you can get to second and sometimes you have to have some help to do it. Maybe that's what all of us have to do—do good and necessary things and help others to do it, too. Maybe that's what makes life worth living. It sounds like the three necessities are a good place to start."

There was a long wave of silence. Finally, Little Bull spoke.

"Hey, J.D.! That's really good!"

"Way to go, J.D.! You really nailed it!" Ralph exclaimed.

Others joined in and some ran over to Jimmy Dan and shook his hand.

Lisa smiled at Graham who told everyone to take their seats.

"Well, Mr. Graham," she chuckled. "Do you have any thoughts?"

Gray ran his hands across his text, grinned at the class and looked at Jimmy Dan.

"I think we all learned something today. Thanks, J.D. Sometimes students are the best teachers."

Suddenly, he whirled and pointed at Jimmy Dan.

"Food, clothing and shelter!" J.D. shouted.

CHAPTER FOURTEEN

ELECTION PLAN

The Citation school experienced few dull moments nor did the community with an election coming up. This time it focused on Bill Sanders.

Sanders ran a dry goods store at the junction. He was a deacon in the Baptist Church, known to be "as honest as the day is long" and had served as a justice of the peace. And, he had been a headache for the county judge and school board.

When he served as JP, Bill had no patience with reckless drivers. Repeated speeding offenses meant a heavy fine and several days in jail. Several school board officials and even County Judge Carson Wells had felt the sting of his wrath.

Wells never forgot the humiliation of his jail time and vowed that Sanders never would serve another term. And Bill didn't. But, now, he was a candidate for the school board.

The judge and Jack Nixon were furious.

"It's the work of that damn Gray Graham!" Wells raged. "Sanders has been one of his allies from day one! We can't have this!"

Nixon growled in agreement.

"Sanders went door to door in the last election to solicit votes for Owen Noland. Those voters went for Noland and this time they'll go for Sanders. That turnout and the Citation school vote would be enough to get Sanders elected. If the school people get two of their own on the board, that's the beginning of a revolution."

"You're preaching to the choir, Nixon!" Wells shouted. "How are we going to stop it!"

"Let's get our man Rossi in the mix," he suggested. "We know that Graham is behind all this and it won't hurt to give him another warning. If that doesn't work, we'll have to stuff the ballot boxes like we did at Brushy Fork."

Wells rubbed his chin as he reflected.

"I don't know. There's still some suspicion about what happened at the Fork. We won by too big a margin."

"We'll make it closer this time," Nixon stated. "But it may not come to that. Maybe we just have to make Graham an offer he can't refuse."

"Like what?"

"Let's leave that to Rossi," Nixon smiled.

Graham still walked the railroad tracks home when the school day concluded, but, since being a shooting target, he was considerably more cautious. He was startled by the call behind him.

"Hey, hold it!"

The order came from a rugged looking miner who appeared to have faced adversity more than once. And, he had faced it head on.

"I need to talk with you. My name's Fred Burden."

"You're Bernice's husband," Gray recognized. "You're the one who stole our library money."

"Yeah, and I'm here to apologize," Fred stated. "When I get drunk I do all sorts of crazy things. I act before I think. When I sobered up, I knew I had to put things right. I can't begin to tell you how glad I am that you got the money back and really sorry you had to do it the hard way.

"Taking on that pool shark is worse than shooting yourself in the foot. I want you to know that you can call on me if you ever need any help. I owe you double. Once for myself and another for my daddy."

Graham frowned.

"I'm not sure what you mean. What's your father got to do with this?"

"It's about paying a debt. Your daddy did mine a favor years ago and my dad never paid him back. I'm here to make things right—for what I did and to repay the favor."

"You've got to explain that," Gray said.

"My dad was Omar Burden. He couldn't hold his liquor any better than I can. Years ago, he got drunk and got into an argument that went bad. He pulled a gun and threatened to shoot the other man. Nobody was hurt, but the sheriff arrested Omar and ordered your dad, who was a deputy sheriff, to take him to jail for disturbing the peace.

"They were on the way when your father stopped and told my dad he couldn't do it. He said, 'Omar, we've known each other all our lives. I don't feel right about putting you in jail. If you promise me you won't run off and will be here in the morning to face the judge, I'll let you go home.'"

"Did Omar show up?" Graham asked.

"He did, but he never got a chance to thank your father. Your dad died soon after, and that preyed on my dad's conscience until the day he died."

Graham cleared his throat.

"That's quite a story. I never knew that."

"So, I'm here to help," Burden continued. "If you get in a bind, you can count on me."

"I may have to do that," Gray acknowledged. "Judge Wells and Jack Nixon have it in for me, and if they had it their way I'd be run out of town. I know about the shooting and I can't help but wonder if they aren't behind it. Whoever it was, I think they were just trying to scare me. I was a target hard to miss."

Burden laughed.

"You're not one to scare easy. Bernice told me that. And let me tell you this. All you need to do if anybody tries that again is to let me know. I'll make them pay for it."

"Thanks, Fred, but I don't want anyone to get killed. I hope it won't come to that."

"If they made their play once, more than likely they'll do it again. I've been in shootouts before and I'm not afraid to take on the devil himself."

"Take it easy, Fred. You kill someone and you're likely to go to prison. I don't want that."

Burden grinned.

"You worry too much, Graham. I don't have any notches on my pistol, but I could have. And I also have this."

With that, Fred reached into his work boot and extracted a custom-made knife. Gray asked to examine it. It had a five-inch blade, a cord-braided handle and was lightweight and perfectly balanced.

"I asked a blacksmith to make me a good throwing knife," Burden explained. "He did a good job. Watch this."

Fred threw the knife at a nearby tree sticking the blade halfway in. He retrieved the weapon and walked back to Gray.

"I don't take any prisoners," he declared, "and I haven't been caught yet."

CHAPTER FIFTEEN

FOREWARNING

Martha Graham had found a good friend in Eileen Branscomb. Eileen lived just down the clubhouse hall from the Grahams and she and Martha usually saw one another at breakfast and often had lunch together.

Eileen was several years younger and often asked Martha for her opinions and advice. As a beautiful single woman, the young nurse had many admirers, but there were few young unmarried men near her age in the coalfield area. Boyd Palmer was the exception.

"Martha, you really don't like Boyd, do you?"

The question came out of the blue as the two women and young Jack Graham were walking to the company store. Eileen and Boyd were dating and the good-looking, flashy dressing Palmer was enough to sweep women off their feet.

Martha thought carefully before answering.

"Oh, I wouldn't say that. But, I'd be careful if I were you."

Puzzled, Eileen frowned as she replied.

"Why, what's wrong with him?"

"Maybe nothing, but he's really out of place here. Boyd's father is a really successful businessman over at the junction, and my husband says he has money to burn. Boyd supposedly works for his father, but he seems to spend most of his time gambling and having fun."

"You're saying that because of that fancy car he drives," Eileen commented.

Palmer had a used Stutz Bearcat that his father had purchased for him in Huntington. It was yellow in color and too fast for the crooked

Eastern Kentucky roads. But that didn't hamper Boyd's style. He drove and lived the same way, with reckless abandon.

Boyd carried a sizeable bankroll and was armed with a blackjack and a .38 police revolver. He fancied the weapons because of an obsession with the roles of actor George Raft. The film star used the club and handgun in many of his gangster movies and Palmer chose to emulate him.

The sap was contained in Boyd's coat pocket and the pistol was secured in a shoulder holster. They were potentially more lethal due to Palmer's quick temper.

Eileen's naïveté was a concern. Martha weighed her words carefully.

"Oh, Eileen, you're my best friend. I just don't want anything bad to happen to you. Boyd is a real charmer. But, he's impulsive and wants to do things his way. Just be careful, that's all."

Selkirk Mining had built Citation conscientiously with three thoughts in mind: make it a decent place to live and work, treat employees and their families right and, of course, make a profit. The company store met the first two criteria with flying colors. Selkirk didn't inflate prices on products and goods and tried to stock whatever the miners and their families and other company employees might need. Even such things as refrigerators and washing machines were available.

On this particular day, Martha was looking for a washing machine. A green wringer washer caught her eye.

"Look at this, Eileen," she said. "I think this would be perfect. What do you think?"

Running her hands over the machine, Eileen's smile indicated she agreed. But, in afterthought, she had a question.

"Where would you put it, Martha? You don't have that much wash-room in your apartment and the storage areas are full. And where would you hang the wet clothes?"

She was right. All second floor tenants shared space in the storage areas and a washing machine couldn't be made to fit. She could rig a clothesline in the one-room apartment, but that would take up all the living space. Also, the machine price was a bit more than she wanted to pay.

Letha Bradbury came to the rescue. She was the wife of Dr. Stephen Bradbury, the company physician. The Bradburys and their daughter, Lisa, were in the process of moving from the clubhouse to a residence they had rented near the junction.

"I overheard you and Eileen and maybe I can help," she offered. "I'd be willing to go half-and-half on the price if we could put the machine in our house. We could set up a washday schedule that would work for both of us. How about it?"

Eileen nudged Martha with her elbow, encouraging her to agree. Both knew Letha well, and it was an arrangement that could work. Martha pondered a moment.

"Okay, but let's be sure our husbands approve."

"That's a deal!" Letha laughed, giving Martha a hug.

Clarissa, a clerk at the store, agreed to put the washer on hold. Letha left, but Martha and Eileen stopped to view some canned goods.

"Hello, ladies."

Eileen's heart skipped a beat when she turned to look at Vito Rossi. He was undeniably handsome, and his features were topped off by an impressive smile. A more subdued Martha observed how thrilled Eileen was to see a good-looking male her own age. Rossi stepped closer to Eileen and caressed her cheek.

"I'd like to get to know you better," he said.

"Excuse us," Martha interrupted, instinctively reaching to clasp Jack's hand. "We were just leaving."

"That's a good-looking boy you have there, Mrs. Graham," Rossi said.

"I'm sorry, do I know you?"

Ignoring Martha query, he kneeled in front of the boy.

"What's your name, son?" Rossi smiled.

"Jack, Jack Graham. What's your name?"

"I'm Vito and I'm very pleased to meet you. This must be your mother and that beautiful girl next to her must be your big sister."

Eileen blushed and covered her mouth.

"No," Jack said. "She's a nurse. Her name is Eileen."

"A beautiful girl with a beautiful name," Rossi declared. "Gray Graham is your daddy, isn't he?

"Do you know my daddy?"

"No, I don't, but I know a lot about him. Your daddy is quite a man. He's got a lot of friends, but some people think he does more than he should. It's too bad some of my friends don't like him very much."

Martha pulled Jack away.

"Let's go," she said. "We have to leave."

Vito stood, his smile gone.

"Don't be rude, Mrs. Graham. Your son and I were just beginning to get acquainted. I'm sorry you have to leave so quickly. We need more time to get to know one another.

"But, if you have to go, know this! It would be a shame if something were to happen to young Jack here. Tell your husband not to anger those in power. It wouldn't be healthy for your youngster, or, maybe even for your husband."

Rossi raised a finger as he stepped away.

"Those shots at the tracks were Graham's first warning. This is his second."

CHAPTER SIXTEEN

DECISION TIME

The sound of gunfire was not uncommon in and around Citation. On election day it usually happened as the county political machine celebrated a sure win after the polls closed. But it was happening now as voters traveled to the polls and it was unnerving as some of the projectiles were too close for comfort.

This time it was a ploy by the machine to influence the vote. This election day, however, was one of malcontent for Judge Wells and Jack Nixon as one of the polling places was at the Citation school.

"Dammit, Judge, how many more advantages do these school people get?" Nixon groused. "Voting there promotes voting for the Citation candidate."

"I'm not happy about it," Wells acknowledged. "I lobbied with the Board of Elections to choose another polling place, but the school was the best location and best size for the precinct. The board also thinks it's appropriate to decide a school board race at a school building. But no matter. We have to win this race by hook or crook."

"Don't worry, I'll take care of it," Nixon said.

The weather was good and the voter turnout was great. But despite their optimism for the outcome, the supporters of Bill Sanders realized they were opposing a long-time winning machine. When it came to vote buying, the Wells-Nixon machine knew the ropes.

Fred Burden worked outside the school, encouraging voters to support Sanders. By mid-morning, he was aware the opposition was gaining control. On the outskirts of the school, he saw voters transported in and out and being rewarded with a half-pint and a dollar-enhanced handshake. And, there was talk about the gunfire. Rumors circulated that sniper gunfire was scaring away some en route to the polls.

Burden fortified himself with several half-pints of his own and began pacing along the lines of voters, his temper raging and his determination to even the odds increasing. Several state policemen were at the school, having investigated the sniper fire incidents. Fred kept pacing and nipping at his bottle.

"What the hell are you doing standing around here!" he roared at the peace officers. "Get out there and make some arrests! Those SOBs are violating the rights of our voters and over there," he pointed, "they're buying votes against us!"

The officers eyed Fred, but made no move. Fred kept drinking and pacing, narrowing his space between the two and himself with each pass.

"That's it! Stand there and do nothing!" he cried. "I'm going to get my gun and handle this myself! I'm not going to let Wells and Nixon steal another election! Now's your chance to throw down on me! Or, are you too bought and paid for to make a move?"

Gray and Charley Fitzpatrick intercepted Fred as his tirade was becoming more confrontational where the two lawmen were concerned.

"Settle down, Fred!" Gray urged. "We need you back inside."

"Let go of me!" he bellowed. "I'm going to my car and get my gun! I've been fighting this damn machine all my life and they've beat me for the last time! I'm sick and tired of it! I'm going to kill me one of these SOBs before this day's over!"

Gray grabbed Fred by the shoulders and shook him.

"Dammit, Fred, stop it! You're going to get us in a gunfight and get us all killed! You've got to sober up and help us win this election. I've got a job for you."

They dragged Burden up the steps and into an adjacent classroom. Gray found a coffee pot and Charley began forcing Fred to drink.

They loosened Fred's shirt collar and began massaging his shoulders. Glancing at Graham, Charley asked, "What do you mean we've got a job for Fred?"

"Why not let him serve as a clerk?"

Paper ballots had to be signed on the back by a clerk and a sheriff's deputy to be valid.

"Hell, he's too drunk to sign his name," Charley noted.

"Let's keep working with him," Gray instructed.

Multiple cups of coffee later, Fred was put to work. He signed the ballots, but kept complaining about the machine buying votes.

"So what," Charley whispered, "so are we. I'm just worried they're outspending us. Keep signing."

At the end of the day, ballot boxes were delivered to Earl Barnes, an attorney and election official, who was in charge of counting the ballots.

Gray, Charley and Fred were standing in the hall eager to get the results. Earl, an anti-machine advocate, exited the vote-counting room, quietly closed the door and motioned to the trio to join him farther down the hall.

"We're in trouble, boys," he murmured. "We're losing and it's going to get worse when we get to the absentee ballots. Wells and Nixon are experts at forging absentee names.

"We ought to do something about it. I'm not telling you what to do. It's just too bad if we can't fix it."

Fred punched a fist against the wall.

"I knew it!" he declared. "They were buying votes with a bankroll that would choke a horse!"

"It's late and we're going to close up for the night," Barnes announced. "We won't resume until tomorrow morning."

Gray and Charley left, but Fred lingered, waiting until the vote counters departed. He wasn't going to lose again.

Classes were back in session the following day and rumors were circulating that Bill Sanders had lost. Gray tried to raise everyone's spirits, reminding the Citation clan that it wasn't over until the last vote was counted. Maybe they'd lose this battle, he told himself, but not the war.

Graham left the school building at four o'clock and drove to the junction to see Sanders. Bill was waiting on customers and receiving well wishes for a victory. He'd heard the rumors, however, and was expecting the worst. He perked up when he saw Gray enter the store.

"Hope you're bringing some good news," he said.

Gray shrugged and held up his palms.

"The last I heard they were still counting absentee ballots," he replied. "The turnout was bigger than we thought and the absentee vote was tremendous. I guess it's going to take a while. There's no need to be discouraged."

Sanders shook his head.

"I've been there before, Gray. Absentee ballots are not good news. I had my last justice race won before the absentees were totaled. The machine knows how to get it done."

The door banged open and an excited Charley Fitzpatrick ran to them.

"I just got the news! It was close, but Bill you won! And that means a big win for the school! Congratulations!"

Handshakes, hugs and laughter were in abundance before Gray asked if Charley knew the margin of victory.

"You won't believe it! We won by four votes!"

Graham was startled. How could that be?

CHAPTER SEVENTEEN

BOYD

"Oh look, Gray, there's Eileen. Who's that she's with?'

Martha Graham motioned toward her friend, Eileen Branscomb, who was some distance ahead exiting the theater with a young man whose back was to them.

"It's Boyd Palmer," Gray answered. "You know him."

"Yes," Martha said in a sad tone. "The one with that gaudy car. I wish Eileen would stop seeing him. He's a little too fast for her."

The Grahams, with young Jack in tow, were leaving the company theater. They'd just seen a George Raft movie, and Gray wasn't surprised that Palmer was in attendance. His fascination with the dapper film star was well known.

Martha caught Eileen's eye and waved. Eileen returned the gesture and spoke to her escort. They smiled at the Grahams and motioned for them to "come over."

Boyd was his usual charming self. After shaking hands with Gray and complimenting Martha on her appearance, he kneeled to shake hands with their youngster.

"I bet you're Jack," he said. "I'm Boyd. Did you like the movie?"

"It was okay. I really liked what that man was throwing up in the air and catching."

Palmer raised a finger and smiled. He pulled a half-dollar from his pocket.

"You must mean this," he winked. "And this is what he did with it!"

Mimicking Raft, Boyd flipped the coin and caught it.

"How did you do that?" Jack marveled.

"You place it on two fingers like this and put your thumb on top. Then you twist your fingers real fast and flip it like this."

Boyd caught the coin and placed it in Jack's hand.

"You take this and practice at home. I'll bet you'll learn to do it just like that movie star."

Martha smiled at Boyd and shook her head.

"Thank you, you're very kind. But this is too much. Jack, give the coin back to Mr. Palmer and say thank you."

"No need, Mrs. Graham. Think of this as a gift. Eileen told me about that trouble you had at the company store. Someone needs to teach that low-life who confronted you a lesson, and I'd like to be the one to do it."

Martha cleared her throat.

"It WAS very uncomfortable," she agreed.

"Threats always are," Boyd said, "and this loser was way out of line. No one should speak to ladies that way," he snapped, "and no one puts his hands on my girl!"

"I'm just glad nobody got hurt, Boyd," Gray said. "Let's let it go at that."

Palmer's eyes turned to steel.

"Not a chance! He was coming on to her!"

"Please stop, Boyd," Eileen pleaded. "You're going to make a scene."

Palmer took a deep breath. They were just a few steps away from the clubhouse.

"Martha, why don't you and Eileen go on ahead and we'll meet you there in a few minutes," Gray suggested.

He took Boyd's arm and guided him to the side.

"Look, Boyd, I'm asking you not to bring up this incident to Martha again. She's worried about Jack's safety and it's taken me a while to get her calmed down. This was just another scare attempt by the judge and his cronies."

Palmer stared in disbelief.

"You're not taking this seriously are you? Well, you should, but that's your business. He didn't threaten Eileen, but he wanted to make out with her. That's an insult to her and to me and I'm making that my business.

"Eileen said he was dark headed, had dark eyes and was average in size. That's not much to go on, but someone must have seen him."

"Okay, Boyd, if you're going to make an issue out of this you might talk with Letha Bradbury or some of the clerks at the store," Graham suggested. "There's also a chance that Harve Martin could be of help."

Harvey Martin was Citation's chief of police. Since Harve was Selkirk's only lawman, his title was a bit of a misnomer, but he was aware of any misconduct in the mining community. And he was quick to ride herd on any wrongdoer.

"Thanks, Mr. Graham," Palmer said. "I appreciate your help, but I think you're making a mistake not to be concerned for your family and yourself. But if I catch up to this guy, he'll never bother Eileen or anyone else again."

The next morning Palmer sought out Harvey Martin. Harve expressed concern about the incident, but had no knowledge about the individual in question.

"There is one thing," he told Boyd. "He could be one of the marshals over at Brushy Fork."

The Brushy Fork mine was south of the junction. Each mining community had its own administrative organization, including its law enforcement staff. Brushy Fork had several marshals, some of whom were recommended and provided by Jack Nixon.

Palmer wheeled his Bearcat in front of the Brushy Fork administrative offices in a shower of cinders and gravel. In his best arrogant style, he made sure his entrance would not go unnoticed. A long-barreled .38 was stuffed in his waistband along with a snub-nosed model anchored in an ankle sheath. These were in addition to the pistol in his shoulder holster. He was outfitted for war.

With a weapon in hand, Boyd kicked open the door and confronted a petite young woman.

"Where's your police chief?" he demanded.

Too shocked to speak, she motioned to another office.

"Bring him in here!" he ordered.

She ran to a nearby cubicle, closing the door after her. Palmer followed, flattened himself against the wall of the entrance, hidden from anyone who would exit. With a backhanded motion, he slammed his pistol into the chief's face as he came into view. He then shoved the weapon under the policeman's chin.

"Where's your enforcer," he demanded, "the one who manhandled my girl?"

"What in hell are you talking about?" the chief groaned. "You broke my nose!"

Boyd jerked him to his feet.

"Get your men in here!"

"They're outside."

"Then let's go get 'em!"

Palmer shoved the chief outside as two men approached. Boyd swung his pistol toward them and they reached for theirs. Palmer shot the nearest man and felt the chief wrench as the law officer took the return fire from his deputies.

Using the chief as a shield, he pulled him to the ground and fired at the second marshal who took refuge behind a coal car. The first man was down and writhing in pain. Boyd emptied one pistol and continued firing with another when a call came from his target.

"I'm out of bullets," he shouted, "and I'm leaving. We'll finish this later."

When convinced that his opponent had departed, Boyd shoved the chief away and walked slowly to his car. The two Brushy Fork officers were wounded, but would get no help from Palmer.

"Who are you?" the chief cried, holding his bloody side.

"Someone after revenge. I'll be back."

CHAPTER EIGHTEEN

DEAD OR ALIVE

Five o'clock.

Gray was startled at the hour showing on the hall clock.

The Citation principal, busy with administrative work, had lost track of the time. He'd been playing catch up for nearly two hours and needed to leave for the clubhouse right away if he were to have dinner with Martha and Jack. Fortunately, he'd driven to work that day and was only minutes away from his destination.

He locked his office and the school building's front door, then paused. He had an intuitive sense that something was amiss. When he reached the foot of the steps he saw why. There was a problem, and it was in the form of Jim Clayton.

Arms folded, Clayton leaned against a battered pickup truck with a brakeman's club in his hand. He had parked his truck against the rear bumper of Graham's vehicle, blocking its exit.

Gray approached cautiously.

"What do you want, Clayton?"

"You know what I want," he said. "I told you I'd clean your plow one day. Today's the day."

Gray slipped off his coat and removed his tie. He rolled up his sleeves as he spoke.

"If you're sure you want to try, put down that billy club. Let's go heads up, no weapons."

Clayton sneered and smacked the club against the palm of his other hand.

"Not a chance! Your head is going to have more dents in it than my truck."

He charged, but Graham ducked under the club swing and drove a hard right into his opponent's stomach before stepping aside. A surprised Clayton stumbled and fell. Rolling quickly to his feet, he raised the club over his head and charged again. The quicker Gray also charged and threw his body against the bigger man's ankles. Clayton skidded head first across the cinder-filled parking area, his face and hands ripped by the uneven surface.

Graham backpedaled and tripped over a pile of rubble, wood scraps from construction of the school building. He reached back to break his fall and his hands closed around a wooden pole, one of several used for cloakroom coat rods. One end had been broken, but it still had a length of nearly five feet.

Struggling to his feet, Gray raised the pole defensively as an enraged Clayton came at him again. He chopped at Graham's head, but the blow was parried. Gray then snapped the end of the stick against Clayton's head and the big man fell again, losing his club.

Dazed, but furious, Clayton made another charge only to be stopped as Graham slapped his weapon across his opponent's face. Clayton took the stunning blow across his forehead. He staggered, but refused to fall. Wiping the blood with a shirt sleeve, he took time to contemplate his next move.

He stepped on a fist-sized rock, picked it up and threw it at Gray, who ducked and pointed the pole at Clayton. The big man charged into the broken end of the pole, which penetrated his left side. It was a bloody flesh wound that hurt and brought him to a halt. The injury was sufficient for him to realize this may not be a battle he could win.

Vito Rossi sat on the hillside just above the parking area. He had made his way down the hill with the intention of assassinating Graham when he left the school building. He stopped short when he saw Clayton drive up, block Graham's car and stand waiting for the school principal to show.

This was too good to be true. It was Jack Nixon's Plan B at its best. Instead of killing Graham and framing Clayton, all Rossi had to do was watch Clayton do the job himself. But who would have thought that a schoolteacher could handle himself so well. Rossi now was worried that Clayton wasn't in good enough condition to finish the job.

It was time for him to make it happen.

The two combatants had paused, several yards apart and breathing hard. The slow but steady sound of clapping hands caught their attention. Rossi continued to slowly clap as he approached.

"Great fight! Great fight! Don't believe either could beat Joe Louis, but you're good against each other."

Too tired and winded to speak, they stared at the Italian hit man.

"You don't look too good, Mr. Clayton," Rossi observed. "You didn't expect Mr. Graham to be this good and, frankly, neither did I."

Clayton wiped blood and perspiration from his eyes and held a dirty bandana against his side. He glared at Rossi.

"Who in the hell are you?"

"Someone who knows you both, but neither of you know me. It's well known, Mr. Clayton, that you have an intense dislike for Mr. Graham and have threatened to … how was it you said? ... oh, yes … you intended to 'clean his plow.'

"Well, in all honesty, I think you should. But you're not doing it very well. If I were you, I'd find another way. Any thoughts?"

"What in hell are you talking about?" Clayton snarled.

"There are other ways to defeat an opponent," Rossi suggested. "You might have a solution inside your truck."

Clayton returned a blank look. Rossi pointed a finger toward him and levered his thumb in the motion of a pistol hammer. He snapped the thumb against his finger and mouthed the word, "Pow!" There was instant understanding.

Moving unsteadily to his truck, Clayton withdrew a .38 stashed beneath the seat. He spun the cylinder, noting that it was fully loaded. He turned to face Graham, who had waited too long for Clayton's next move.

"Go ahead," Rossi urged. "Let him have it!"

"Shut up!" Clayton shouted. "I've had enough of your yammering!"

He turned the pistol on Rossi and fired. He missed and the hit man ran behind the pickup truck. He kept shooting at Rossi until a final round clicked on empty. As he began to reload, the Italian withdrew his weapon and calmly shot Clayton in the head.

Holding his pistol to the side, Rossi walked toward Graham, who raised his long baton into a defensive position.

"I guess I'm next," Gray observed.

"No, not today schoolteacher," Rossi replied. "When plans don't come together, you live to fight another day. But, you're still on my list. I'll be seeing you."

"Who are you?" Gray demanded.

"Someone who would rather see you dead than alive. No offense intended, however."

Rossi trudged back up the hill.

CHAPTER NINETEEN

ELIMINATION

Fred Burden remained mum about the election results. Only he, Creed Randall, Pegleg Butcher and Squire Pelfrey knew how Bill Sanders had won.

Late at night after the vote counters had adjourned, Fred jimmied a window and went to work. Armed with a new sheaf of ballots, he and his assistants picked the locks on the ballot boxes, removed the bulk of those supporting the other candidate and replaced them with votes for Sanders. They finished just before dawn and left in a hurry. They had no time to make a count. Burden just hoped for the best.

Cheating had decided many elections in Shawnee County. The important thing was not to be caught. The machine usually won comfortably and, to the best of anyone's knowledge, it had never lost a race by a mere four votes.

Fred had sweated blood awaiting the outcome, but permitted himself only a brief sigh of relief when the results became official. He still had work to do. There was a sniper out there somewhere, and he was determined to find him.

Burden went to the junction and found Boyd Palmer at his father's store. He'd heard about Boyd's scrape at Brushy Fork and was told that both may be after the same man. They exchanged information, still unsure they were seeking the same individual.

"I'll keep looking, and if I have to clean out every dirty nest in the process I'll do it," Boyd declared.

"Just don't get caught," Fred advised.

"I haven't been caught yet."

"Neither have I," Burden replied. "Good luck."

"You too."

The sniper fire directed at Graham and the election-day voters had occurred at the same place—at the railroad tracks some two hundred yards past the school and north toward the Selkirk clubhouse. Fred made his way to the location and, using binoculars, scoured the hillside. He wasn't sure what he was searching for, but became certain nothing would show up from long range. He had to take his chances and walk the danger zone.

The hill was the beginning of a steep incline that ended atop a rocky mountain. West Virginia, the adjoining state, was on the other side of the elevation. A good marksman with a long-range weapon and a scope could control the tracks below if he had an unobstructed view.

Burden, with revolver in hand, inched his way upward and, suddenly, found the spot. Several rocks were placed in front of a scooped out area with a narrow view to the tracks. It was too distant to be noticed from below, but just right above for a well-placed shot from a skilled marksman.

Placing himself in the shooter's lair, it was obvious to Fred that the shots fired at Graham and those walking to the polls were only warnings. Kill shots were available for the taking.

Suddenly, the staccato sounds of a bolt action were followed by a crisp command.

"Drop it!"

Startled, Fred raised his hands, but held on to his pistol.

"Do it or you're a dead man!"

Burden tossed his weapon aside and froze in place.

"Turn around, slow and easy and keep your hands up."

Vito Rossi had his rifle trained on Fred's midsection. A bulbous cylinder was attached to the barrel's muzzle followed by a bipod. It was a mean looking weapon.

"Who are you?" Burden asked.

"Obviously, the man you're looking for," the gunman replied. "The name's Rossi, Vito Rossi. And, you're Fred Burden, the man I've been stalking.

"Also, there's no need to ask the question. Yes, I'm the sniper, the shooter who has been keeping you folks on your toes. The gentlemen who employ me no longer wish to just frighten you. I've been told to eliminate Mr. Graham and, if necessary, terminate his companions. I guess I'll start with you."

Burden grinned, then broke out in laughter.

"Well, I'll be damned! What a way to end it all! I never thought this is the way I'd go!"

Rossi snickered.

"Well, at least you're leaving with a sense of humor. Most of my targets are afraid to die."

"Oh, you do this often?'

"This is what I do for an occupation," Vito explained. "In Detroit, they refer to me as an enforcer. You people describe it as a hit man."

"What are you doing here?"

"You see, I ran into a problem in Detroit and had to leave town quite suddenly. Too many kills too quickly. I work for an organization known as La Cosa Nostra, or, as you call it down here, The Mob. I was told to go south and, when I got here, I found employment as a coal field marshal."

"A professional killer, huh? Why are you using a rifle?"

"I took it off a German gentleman who was a sniper in the war. He was an enforcer for the opposition and didn't need it anymore."

"You killed him?"

"As they say in gangster movies, he asked for it. I gave it to him and found this weapon in his apartment."

"I don't suppose you'd let me examine it," Fred said, "but I'd like to know more about it."

"It's a Mauser army rifle used on the Western Front by a German sniper. It has a silencer, a 4X telescopic sight and a bipod. I can fire five rounds as fast as I can manage the bolt action. After I finish you, I'm going to take out Mr. Graham as he walks home."

"Who else is on your hit list?"

"Well, that young Mr. Palmer for one," Rossi continued. "I got into a gun battle with him at Brushy Fork and ran out of ammunition. I need to get him before he gets me."

Burden straightened and his eyes widened.

"You'd better move, Rossi! There's something coming down the mountain you don't want to face!"

Vito sneered.

"Come on, Burden, you can do better than that. Save your movie dialog for someone else."

Rossi wasn't the snake's target. Black, long and ugly, it passed between his legs. The hit man jumped aside and trained his rifle on the serpent.

Fred moved quickly, withdrew the blade from his high-top shoe and threw it at Rossi. It caught him in the throat.

Vito dropped the rifle, his hands flying to the knife. He fell to his knees as blood gushed from the wound. Unable to speak, he stared in alarm then rolled onto his side.

Burden used his foot to prevent the body's slide downhill. He removed the knife, and grasping Rossi's legs, Fred then began the arduous task of pulling the dead man up hill. He was soaked with perspiration and gasping for breath when he reached the summit. He rested for a while as he studied the other side's descent.

He found the spot he wanted. The rocky slope was devoid of trees, only sparsely punctuated by underbrush, and extended into a wild-looking valley. Rolling the body before him, Fred gave a final shove and the lifeless form bounced and skidded over the terrain until it reached a hidden resting place.

'I've never been caught yet,' Burden mused, 'and I won't be now thanks to West, by God, Virginia.'

CHAPTER TWENTY

OUTDONE

With the death of Rossi, the fireworks, figuratively and literally, were past and Gray was looking forward to days with more regularity. Billy Joe Taylor, however, wasn't about to let that happen.

The eighth grader was caught stealing lunch money from other students by Sarah Webb, his teacher. Sarah said he'd been doing this for some time and she had admonished him repeatedly. But, she related to Graham in frustration, he still was doing it despite the fact that he had lunch money of his own.

"Bring him in," Gray ordered.

Sarah did. But Billy Joe denied the accusation.

"How can you say that when Mrs. Webb caught you in the act?" Gray inquired.

"Maybe she didn't see what she thought she saw," the youngster stated.

"Come on, Billy Joe, Mrs. Webb isn't blind. She's talked with you several times about this, but you keep doing it. Your father gives you lunch money so I know you're not starving. Don't you know it's wrong to steal?"

"Yeah, I guess so," he said.

"Then why are you doing it?"

Billy Joe looked around the room hoping to avoid a response.

"Answer me!" Gray demanded. "Why are you doing it?"

Finally, he gave up.

"I needed it to buy candy," he admitted.

Gray leaned back and studied the student.

"Well, we'll have to do something about this. I'm going to give you a choice. I'll give you a paddling or we'll send you to reform school. You pick. Which one do you want?"

Billy Joe looked Graham in the eye.

"Well, you've paddled me before and if it's all the same to you, I'd just as soon go to reform school."

Sarah was stunned. Gray was speechless.

"Are you sure that's the choice you want to make?" Graham finally asked.

The accused nodded that it was.

"You stay here, Billy Joe," Graham instructed. "Mrs. Webb and I need to step outside and make the arrangements."

Gray forcefully exhaled and Sarah appeared dumbfounded.

"What are we going to do?" she implored. "I wasn't prepared for this!"

"Nor am I," Gray stated.

The principal pondered for a moment.

"Who's that student in your class who has a bicycle?'

"Chip Scott," Sarah said. "He rides it to school every day."

"Let's go see him."

They found Chip in the hallway and Gray pulled him aside.

"I need you to do something," Graham related. "Ride your bicycle over to Mr. McLeod's office and see if they can find Harve Martin. Tell them I need Harve right away."

Sarah returned to her classroom and Clay returned to his office. He sat down facing Billy Joe.

"I've sent for the police chief," he explained, "and Mr. Martin should be here soon. Is there anything else you need to say or tell me?"

"No, I don't guess so," the boy replied.

"Then you wait here and I'll be back with Mr. Martin."

Graham walked outside as the police chief sped up in a rattletrap pickup truck. Chip sat in front with his bicycle in the vehicle's bed.

"What's wrong?" Harve questioned. "I got here just as soon as I could."

Gray explained the situation and told Martin he needed to paint reform school in the worst possible manner. The juvenile was waiting patiently when they entered.

"Billy Joe, this is Harvey Martin," Graham said. "He's here to arrest you."

Billy Joe extended his hands toward the police chief.

"What are you doing?" a puzzled Martin asked.

"Waiting for the handcuffs."

"There's no need to handcuff you," Harve explained. "That is, if you come along peacefully."

"Okay," the youngster replied.

Martin looked at Graham with a demeanor that asked, 'What's next?' Gray cleared his throat and tried another tact.

"Billy Joe, we can't waste any time. We're going to take you to reform school right now. We don't have time to let you see your parents. Do you understand?"

"I guess so," the boy shrugged.

Gray nodded to Martin, a non-verbal request for the chief to think of something.

"I need to tell you, Billy Joe, what you're in for," Harve began. "Reform school is a prison for young people. You will do as you're told and have no freedom to do anything you might like. The food is awful and you may only get two meals a day. You won't have time for lunch because you'll be working at a difficult job, like using a sledgehammer to break up big rocks.

"You'll be locked in a jail cell at night and, if you're lucky, you'll get a bed with a hard mattress. Reform schools are crowded these days and you may have to sleep on the floor. They'll get you up at five in the morning and you'll work until eight o'clock before going to breakfast.

"You'll go to school until noon, then back at work breaking up rocks. Suppertime is around five o'clock and usually is just some moldy bread and water."

Billy Joe frowned.

"No candy, huh?"

Harve shook his head and turned toward Gray.

"I hope you have something to add, Mr. Graham," he pleaded.

"Mr. Martin didn't mention anything about homework," Gray noted. "You'll have assignments that you'll have to do in your cell and you'll only have about two hours to get everything done before they have lights out. You won't have much time to study for tests, but your teacher will expect you to have perfect scores. And, you better be good or you'll have more time added to your sentence. I've known boys who create problems to serve as many as two or three extra years.

"Isn't that right, Mr. Martin?"

"Absolutely!" Harve acknowledged. "Boys who steal usually have to serve at least two years. But, in your case, it might be even more. I just hope your parents won't forget you while you're locked up."

Graham nodded in agreement.

"Parents usually aren't permitted to see their sons who are in reform school. And, if you complain about it, they'll whip you with a big cane stick."

Harve grasped his head with both hands and excluded a loud "whoosh."

"Boy, do they that like that cane pole! They just look for excuses to use it!"

Gray remained skeptical. He didn't think they were convincing.

"You know, Billy Joe, if I were you I'd prefer a paddling here instead of being beaten all the time in reform school. What do you think?"

Billy Joe placed his hands on his knees and rocked back and forth several times.

"No candy and lots of whippings?"

"That's right," Gray replied.

Billy Joe stood, leaned across Graham's desk and projected his rear end.

"Okay," he said, "let's get to it."

CHAPTER TWENTY-ONE

ROOF FALL

As usual, things never were dull at Citation school. Today, it was a rumbling roar accompanied by a vibration that made some things rattle and others to fall. It also interrupted Eula Deaver's math class. She walked to the window as students stood, while some moved to follow.

In the distance, a dust cloud emanated from number two mine and the questions began.

"What was that?" "Are they blasting?" "Is there a cave-in?"

Eula quieted the class and had everyone return to their seats.

"It's probably nothing," she said. "I heard yesterday they would be pulling pillars and that's noisy and dirty work. Let's get back to our assignment."

Pulling pillars meant removing sections of coal that were supporting a mine's roof. It was part of the retreat mining process. When an area was completely mined, ceiling supports were removed and the roof was allowed to collapse. Usable coal was taken from the collapsed pillar, and the activity was repeated while moving toward the mine entrance. It was a noisy procedure, but no reaction like this was usual, Eula reasoned.

Outside, the scene was hectic. Liam McLeod rushed to the site as men with equipment poured into the shaft. Two men, he learned, were trapped by the rock fall. Roof pressure was so great that the collapse created a domino effect on the adjoining pillars, resulting in a catastrophic failure.

McLeod grabbed rescue gear and joined the team trying to get through the mess of stone and dirt. But, it was taking too long. He had experienced mining accidents for many years and recognized this situation as a massive coal burst. Open areas were filled with enormous amounts of debris and its removal lessened the chances of getting to the injured in time. A miracle was required if the miners were to be found alive.

Students and faculty left the building in a hurry as the Citation school day concluded. As one, their destination was the disaster scene. Gray walked the perimeter of the area, making sure not to be in the way of the rescue team. He was about to leave when he saw McLeod seated on a mantrip with a pick and shovel. The vehicle, used to transport miners down to and up from the mine, wouldn't be used anytime soon.

The mine manager was covered with perspiration and coal dust and obviously had been active in attacking roof fall debris himself in addition to supervising rescue activity.

"How bad is it, Mac? Are you making any progress?" Graham asked.

McLeod shook his head and wiped his face with a bandana.

"Naw, this is a bad one," he replied. "Retreat mining always is dangerous and even with our best men, something like this can happen. We'll keep at it until we find the injured, but we have to find them soon."

"Do you know their location?"

"We're not sure," Mac said. "The coal burst was huge and I'm guessing they were some distance from the entrance when the collapse began. They could be really far away."

"Do you know what caused it?"

"A dinnae ken," he growled. "I don't know, but he might."

Mac then pointed to a foreman who was rounding up a fresh rescue unit.

"Ike Wilson was supervising the retreat and left to get more equipment when the collapse occurred. He thought they needed to modify the roof support because of a particular fault line.

"Ike believed one pillar might have been too small in view of the fault."

Gray appeared puzzled.

"You're probably not all that familiar with retreat mining," Mac said. "Once we exhaust a coal deposit you're aware that we leave pillars to provide ceiling support. If the pillars are too small, there's a risk of failure. When that happens the roof squeezes down, crushing the pillars. With the failure of one pillar, the weight on other pillars increases and that causes a chain reaction of pillar failures. This can cause a massive collapse of the mine.

"If Ike was correct about that fault line, it could have slowly expanded and become critical without additional support. If he could have brought in some timbers in time, maybe the collapse could have been avoided.

"But, who knows? If pillars are too small, the mine will collapse, but if they're too large good coal will be left behind. If we had all the answers, no one would be injured and we wouldn't be in this situation today."

McLeod lowered his head and exhaled.

"With the Maker's help and a lot of luck, maybe we can save those poor souls!"

"Do you know who they are?" Gray asked.

"According to Ike, they're Luke Hays and Curtis Montgomery," Mac said. "We checked the disk board and their numbers were missing. They both have sons in your school."

Graham swallowed hard. Their sons were Eldon Hays and Jason Montgomery. They were in the group that had demanded paddling if and when they'd done something wrong.

"Have the families been notified?"

"We've taken them to the clubhouse," Mac stated. "They're with some of their neighbors and they probably won't go home until we know the outcome."

Hours turned into days before the two miners were found. The cheerless mood of the community extended to the school as students and teachers awaited funeral arrangements. Eldon and Jason were absent, tending to the needs of their grieving families.

Following the graveside service, Gray offered his condolences to the families and waited to speak privately with his two students, fifteen-year-olds who'd had to grow up overnight.

"I guess we won't be seeing you much anymore," Eldon said. "Jason and I talked and we agreed that we won't be able to return to school. We're the oldest ones in our families and we need to get jobs to support them."

Jason agreed.

"I've got to take care of my mother and two sisters," he said.

"And I've got my mother, two brothers and a sister to feed," Eldon added.

Gray knew the answers, but asked anyway.

"Where are you going to get jobs?"

"Where else?" they said in unison. "In the mines."

Eldon shook hands with Gray.

"Remember when you talked about the necessities of life?" he asked. "I never realized how important they are and what we may have to do to get them. J.D. said that was just the beginning. You go from there to do better things."

"What Eldon is saying is that we won't be coal miners forever," Jason continued. "You've taught us to be our best. And that's what we're going to do."

CHAPTER TWENTY-TWO

THE CANDIDATE

Carson Wells and Jack Nixon never gave up. Even a mine disaster could not curtail their scheming.

They used every trick in the book to discredit Gray Graham and the Citation school faculty in their quest to bring the coal mining institution under county control. This time their ploy was Avery Buchanan.

Buchanan, a lumber merchant, had been drafted by Judge Wells and County School Board Chairman Nixon to run for state representative. They promised the junction businessman all the financial and political support he would need. All he had to do was promote and push the county political machine's line. And, at Citation, that was acceptance of the school into the county system. If that were accomplished, the Judge and Board Chair could fire Gray and dispose of non-compliant faculty members.

Wells and Nixon worked with Buchanan in developing a speech focused on operating a school like a business. The Citation company theater was rented for a rally supporting their candidate.

The theater was filled with voters from Shawnee County's two precincts and those recruited by Wells' county machine. The Judge and Nixon were optimistic they could make an impact. Buchanan was nice looking, a good speaker and a successful businessman. If anyone could sway support for their ticket, they were confident Buchanan was the man.

"Ladies and gentlemen, you know me," Avery began. "I've been at the junction for nearly fifteen years and I've supplied you and the mines in Shawnee County with first class building materials during all those years.

I'm for you and Shawnee County, and I'm asking you as a candidate for the state legislature to give me your support so I can continue to do what is best for you and this county."

Buchanan continued with superlatives concerning what he could accomplish. He noted that the Depression was not going to last forever and that he could help bring it to an end while providing Shawnee and its citizens with the economic growth it deserved.

"We need to get everyone back to work," he said, "and we need to provide our young people with an education earmarked for success. "They've been provided with the basics here at Citation, but the basics just aren't enough. We need to move the Citation school into the county system where our children can experience those things that are necessary to succeed in the world of tomorrow.

"A vote for me is a vote for the good things that are ahead for Shawnee and our young people," he emphasized. "Help me to help make that happen."

The Judge's entourage stood and broke out in thunderous applause. Buchanan smiled and waved his hands in victory. It went unnoticed that the Citation residents didn't concur.

With his remarks concluded, Buchanan asked for questions. Those recognized were individuals armed with loaded questions supplied by Wells and Nixon. Confident that momentum was on their side, Buchanan began to recognize some unfamiliar participants.

Bernice Burden was one of them.

"Mr. Buchanan," she announced, "I'm Bernice Burden, a resident of Citation and a teacher in the school here. You mentioned that we've provided our students with a basic education, but they need to be a part of the county system to be successful in life. You also mentioned that we need to operate schools like a business. To do those things that are practical and will be profitable in the years ahead."

"That's right, Miz Burden," Avery responded. "Businesses know how to produce quality and provide continuous improvement. Do you have a question?"

"I understand, Mr. Buchanan, that your business provides quality building materials. Is that correct?"

"Absolutely, Miz Burden," he replied. "Our firm has supplied lumber for the homes and businesses throughout Shawnee County. In fact, we supplied the materials to build the residences and offices in Citation, not to mention the fine school where you teach. We're committed to provide the finest in construction supplies."

"Are your building materials really the best?"

"Again, you're absolutely correct." Buchanan smiled. "We provide nothing but the best. That's what good business is all about."

"Your lumber is seasoned and guaranteed to last?"

"No doubt about it. We stand behind our products."

"What if you receive some defective materials. What do you do then?"

"We don't deal in defective merchandise," Buchanan related. "Seconds are not acceptable at my firm. If something doesn't meet our standards, we send it back. In business, quality is paramount."

Bernice clapped her hands and urged others to join in.

"I applaud you, Mr. Buchanan, and I agree. In business, quality is everything. And, if something doesn't measure up, you're right to send it back. But, you see, education doesn't work that way.

"The raw material we work with is our students. We accept them as they are. We take them big, small, rich and poor. We accept them if they're gifted, exceptional and brilliant. Or, if they're abused, frightened and lack self confidence. But, we take them all. We work with them to make them the best they can be.

"It's not easy. We worry that we're not doing enough. We have sleepless nights attempting to find ways to do a better job. And, our reward is not measured in dollars and cents. It's measured in the outcome of those students. Their success is our success.

"We don't send them back. We take them as they are, and, hopefully, we'll turn out a product that everyone can be proud of. We're not a business, we're a school. Some schools are better than others, but I'll put ours at Citation up against any in the county."

The theater exploded. Teachers, principals, custodians and all those who lived in the mining community jumped to their feet and screamed, "Citation! Citation! Citation!"

Buchanan forced a smile as he waved at the crowd while making his way offstage. Wells and Nixon were a picture of gloom warmed over as they saw another plan fail.

Charley Fitzpatrick nudged Gray Graham as they joined in the applause for their teacher.

"Who would have believed it!" he grinned. "Bernice Burden, of all people! What a speech!"

Graham smiled in agreement.
"Maybe we've found our next candidate for the school board."

CHAPTER TWENTY-THREE

ERROR CORAM NOBIS

"Earl, I need your help."

Gray Graham was at the office of attorney and friend Earl Barnes. If one ploy didn't work, the county political machine always seemed to have another to rid itself of the Citation juggernaut and its principal.

"I've been given a ticket for speeding and reckless driving that's bogus," Gray explained, "And I understand the penalty is at least a heavy fine and could even involve some jail time."

"Are you guilty?"

"No. I was driving through the junction and was pulled over by a policeman who said I was exceeding the speed limit and driving erratically. He gave me a ticket and said this was a serious offense. I asked him to explain and he said I had run a stop sign and failed to yield right of way. I objected and, instead of listening, he told me to 'tell it to the judge.' I'm going to fight this and I need you to represent me."

"Was anyone in the car with you?"

"No, I was alone."

"So, no one to vouch for you? No one to support your side of the story?"

"No one," Gray affirmed.

Barnes drummed his fingers on the desk.

"This could be tough," he said, "but if you want to go to court I'll see what I can do."

Earl stroked his chin.

"You know this smacks of being something else, perhaps an action with an ulterior motive. Could this be possible?"

Barnes posed the question with a wink and a knowing look.

"You're thinking what I'm thinking," Clay acknowledged. "Judge Wells would do almost anything to harass me."

The attorney stood and extended his hand.

"Let me have your citation. I'll do some investigation and make some inquiries. I'll be in touch."

The day of the hearing finally arrived. Barnes nudged Graham as they entered the courtroom of the Justice of the Peace.

"Look who's over there!"

Judge Carson Wells was seated by the sidewall. He glared at Graham before turning his attention to the Justice, Ollie Harlow.

The JP quickly dispensed with several cases before motioning to an officer. They spoke in low tones, with Gray receiving several glances during the discussion.

The JP cleared his throat and called for the next case, indicating that it was Graham's turn.

Harlow had a sixth-grade education, was a long-time flunky of Judge Wells and administered a very low grade of justice. Since he was compensated by fees and fines, Harlow was quick to levy substantial penalties and incarceration was ordered for those who gave him any difficulty. His philosophy was that you were guilty, period.

"So you're Graham, the school principal," Harlow observed. "For the record, how do you plead?"

"We're pleading not guilty, your honor," Barnes announced as he stood with Graham and faced Harlow.

Harlow glared over his glasses. "And who the hell are you?"

"I'm Earl Barnes your honor, the attorney representing Mr. Graham."

The judge swiveled his chair and turned to face Carson Wells, who gestured to continue.

"You're really going to try and get out of this with a not-guilty plea?" Harlow asked Graham.

Gray just pointed toward Earl.

"Your honor, may I approach the bench?" Barnes asked.

Harlow turned to gaze at Barnes and studied him for a moment.

"All right," he relented.

"Your honor, we have a problem with this charge," Earl commented as he stood at the rectangular table in front of the seated Harlow. "I've been examining the paperwork and we definitely have a major error in connection with this allegation."

Harlow frowned in obvious disgust.

"This is about as simple a case of wrongdoing as there is," he growled. "Graham, here, broke the law, pure and simple, and he's going to pay for it. We don't have time to waste with a lot of fancy lawyer talk."

"Your honor," Earl responded, "We're not well acquainted, but I can tell you're a man who honors the letter of the law and who has a high regard for justice. Because of this, I know you would not want an innocent man falsely charged."

"What are you getting at?"

"The traffic ticket itself, your honor," Earl explained. "If you'll note, the ticket is made out to a 'John Martin Graham.'"

"Yeah, so what?"

"Well, your honor, perhaps the alleged perpetrator of this traffic violation is another individual named Graham. It's not my client, however."

"What're you talking about?" Harlow snarled.

The judge turned and looked at the police officer.

"Well, Officer Davis, give the man an answer! Point out Graham and let's get on with it!"

Chester Davis was puzzled, but pointed a finger at Gray and said, "That's John Martin Graham there."

"Officer," Earl asked, "are you indicating my client?"

"Yes, I am," Davis acknowledged.

"Then this proves my case, your honor," Earl continued. "This man is John Martin Graybeal Graham, not 'John Martin Graham' as the officer has indicated. It would appear that we have a case of mistaken identity, which would necessitate a request for a writ of error coram nobis."

Harlow glanced at Davis and looked back at Barnes.

"What did you say?"

"I said that it's apparently a case of mistaken identity, which ..."

"No, no, I don't mean that!" Harlow snapped. "What was it you said about a writ of uh-h-h ..."

"A writ of error coram nobis, your honor. As a learned student of the law and the criminal justice system, I'm sure you agree that a request for such a writ certainly is in order. And, if necessary, the court could be requested to issue it forthwith."

Harlow squinted and stared at Barnes. He then looked at Davis. The officer shook his head and shrugged.

"Uh-h-h, would you approach the bench again?" the JP asked Earl.

Barnes gestured to Graham to stay put and approached the judge. Harlow beckoned to Earl to come to the side of the table where they could speak with more privacy.

"Uh-h-h, look counselor, this writ you're talking about. We, uh-h-h, don't have many requests for writs of erra ... ," Durham gestured with his hand as he groped for the words.

"For writs of error coram nobis?"

"Right, right," the judge replied. "Are you sure you want this?"

"Your honor, it isn't a question of whether it's wanted, it's a matter of justification," Earl stated. "I realize, however, as a student of the law that you're aware this situation is not without precedent. And, I'm sure as you consider the merits of this case that I certainly would be within my rights as Mr. Graham's counsel to request a writ of error coram nobis.

"After all," Earl smiled, "I'm sure you prefer your court to serve as coram rege in this situation."

Harlow's expression was blank as Barnes spoke. He sat for several seconds with the expressionless look, then blinked and snapped back his head as if in complete agreement.

"Of course, of course," he nodded and motioned for Earl to return to where Gray was seated.

Harlow cracked his gavel against the table and announced, "We'll have a brief recess to consider counsel's request."

He motioned to Davis and Judge Wells and they left the area that served as a courtroom and went to an office shared by the mayor and city clerk.

"What in hell is that writ request!" Wells shouted in a tone so loud it was heard outside the office. "And dammit, Ollie, make these people talk American!"

Harlow was heard questioning Davis and books of some weight were pulled from shelves and plopped on desks. In a few minutes, Lonzo Baker, who served as the city attorney, walked in and hurriedly headed for the office. More conversation followed.

A short time later, the office door opened and a grim Harlow headed for the long table that served as his bench. Davis and a puzzled Baker sat in chairs near a red-faced Judge Wells, who was mad enough to bite a nail in half.

Harlow beckoned Earl to again approach the bench.

"I've talked this case over with the police and the city attorney," the judge explained, "and I think we've reached an agreement. I don't see any need for a writ of erra cora nobles. Instead, I think we'll just dismiss the charges with a warning to Mr. Graham."

He motioned for Gray to come forward.

"Mr. Graham," Harlow commented, "I suggest that you watch yourself when you're driving around here. I—the court, that is—don't hold with reckless driving.

"Case dismissed!"

Gray grabbed Earl's hand as they stepped outside.

"Where did you come up with that Latin writ and those phrases?"

"It's old English law," Barnes replied. "A writ of error coram nobis dates back to the early 1200s—or earlier—when the King of England was asked to intervene in correcting errors that may have been made in lower courts. Error coram nobis is a writ concerning an error in fact, which, in your case, was an error in the way your name appeared on the traffic ticket. By writing 'John Martin Graham' instead of 'John Martin Graybeal Graham' a mistake was made by the officer. He failed to write your name in full as it appears on your driver's license. And that raises a question as to whom was being charged—you or someone else."

"Does that mean a writ of error coram nobis was justified?" Gray asked.

"Why don't you ask the judge?"

Graham snorted, "I think I'll pass."

"But," he continued, "what about 'coram rege?' What's that mean?"

"Again, that's old English law," Earl explained. "Coram rege was a tribunal that reviewed miscarriages of justice and unlawful procedures. Judge Harlow's court doesn't necessarily qualify as a coram rege, but I don't think he was aware of that."

Gray grinned. "I think he'll remember erra cora nobles."

Earl grinned back. "That's easy for you to say."

"But a lot easier for Justice Harlow," Graham replied.

Judge Wells was at it again. The sound of his rants and raves extended beyond the building.

"Davis, you idiot!" he screamed. "How could you be so stupid to make a mistake with Graham's name?"

The officer gave a sheepish reply.

"I didn't know anybody had three first names."

CHAPTER TWENTY-FOUR

THE PAGEANT

Despite ongoing political interferences, the Citation community was well planned and developed. But it was missing one thing—a church.

The nearest religious facility was a Baptist church at the junction and, despite the long walk, a number of Citation families attended services there. But the minister, Walker Hager, wanted to do more. He began conducting services once a month in the company theater, and was pleased at the turnout.

As Christmas drew near, Rev. Hager was approached about conducting a seasonal pageant involving the children. He asked Martha Graham and Eileen Branscomb to organize it. Martha was reluctant, but Eileen was elated.

"Oh, come on, Martha!" the nurse exclaimed. "It'll be exciting. You direct it and I'll make the costumes! This will be lots of fun!"

"And lots of work," Martha commented. "I've done this before."

"We don't have to make it a big extravaganza," Eileen said, "just a simple manger scene with Mary, Joseph and the wise men."

"You have to keep a pageant simple," Martha agreed, "but even at that, anything that can go wrong probably will. You have to find students willing to perform and get someone to build a manger set. And that's if you just hold it to Mary, Joseph and the three wise men."

"But we have to have at least two shepherds, some angels and someone to do the narration and a pianist," Eileen added. "And it would be great to have a few sheep and a donkey for Mary to ride in on. Then, we could …"

"Hold it, hold it! You're already creating an accident that's just waiting to happen. Animals are hard to manage and where are you going to find sheep and a donkey?"

"No problem," Eileen beamed. "There's a donkey in town that was used once in the mines and they have sheep at the Harrison farm near the junction."

"That donkey is worn out and blind," Martha explained, "and the Harrison farm won't loan out animals they're either going to shear or slaughter.

"The last pageant I attended was a disaster. They had a donkey and sheep and they were a problem from the very start. The donkey refused to be led, shook Mary off in the aisle and the sheep had diarrhea. Joseph stepped in the feces, slipped and fell causing the sheep to run into the audience. The wise men chased them, the manger was destroyed and one of the piano's legs was broken as the accompanist was playing 'O, Holy Night.'

"On top of that, the doll portraying the Baby Jesus was lost and it took two weeks to air out the church. Do you see why I don't think a pageant is a good idea?"

"You're an alarmist, Martha!" Eileen charged. "You've directed plays at the school and they've been a huge success. Together, we can do this. We can bring the spirit of Christmas to a community that really needs it. How about it?"

She grasped Martha's arm and offered a pleading expression that was impossible to resist. Martha sighed and embraced her friend.

"Okay, I give up," she said. "It's against my better judgment, but let's do it."

Eileen squealed with delight.

"Let's go to the company store and find some materials for costumes!"

Martha rolled her eyes, second-guessing her decision.

Eileen's enthusiasm knew no bounds. She convinced the store management to donate material for Mary's garment and that of the angels, and some sheets that could be cut and concocted into headdresses for Joseph and the wise men. Robes, they advised, could be bathrobes.

A small packing crate that could serve as a crib was added, along with some shipping skids for construction of a manger backdrop. Discarded rubber tubing could be devised into halos for the angels.

"Now, all we need is some straw," Eileen smiled. "I'll help find student actors, but I bet you already know some from school plays. See, this isn't going to be so hard after all."

Martha developed a simple script and wrote speaking parts only for Mary and the wise men. The cast of second-graders, however, was greater than she desired. She simplified arrangements by having the two angels and the shepherd duo stand in place around the set. Eileen had insisted on the angel-shepherd parts, and Martha was fortunate to limit the number.

The narrator would read that part of the scripture concerning the journey to Bethlehem by following the star in the east. The wise men would walk down the aisle during the voice over while a light with a star façade was illuminated over the set. The pianist would play when the wise men exited.

Eileen had made the costumes and supervised the set and star construction by Selkirk volunteers. Everything was ready for a final dress rehearsal and, surprisingly, Martha thought it went well. She spent some extra time with Mary and the wise men as they memorized their lines.

Martha sat in the front row, and Eileen was with the wise men to start them down the aisle. They were halfway to the manger when the gold-bearer remembered he'd forgotten his gift. He ran back to retrieve it as the star in the east began to flicker and quit functioning.

He sped back to the set flustered and somewhat breathless. He was to say, "We come bearing gifts for the baby in swaddling clothes." But, it didn't come out that way. Instead, he said the infant was "wrapped in swatting clothes."

Mary immediately objected. "That's wrong, silly! You're supposed to say he's wrapped in squatting clothes."

The wise man didn't like being corrected and got into a wrestling match with Mary. In the process, one of the angels had her halo bent and the other lost a wing.

Eileen had moved to the back of the set and ran forward to restore order. She then prompted the second wise man to speak his part.

"We bring gifts of gold, Frankenstein and fur," he said.

Mary was incensed and picked up the doll representing the Baby Jesus. In her haste, she dropped it and it rolled between the legs of the third wise man. He picked it up and Mary grabbed for it. Unfortunately, she jerked off its head. Martha quickly cued the pianist as the audience convulsed in laughter.

As the crowd left, Martha sought to comfort a crestfallen Eileen.

"Cheer up," she urged. "So it didn't go as planned. But the audience loved it."

"I guess you're right," Eileen shrugged. "We've given them a Christmas they'll never forget."

CHAPTER TWENTY-FIVE

THE CAMPAIGN

There were more than thirty bullet holes in Bill Sanders' Ford coupe when it was towed back to the junction. Miraculously, Sanders escaped injury by diving out of the car and into a brush-covered ditch when the gunfire began. His sniper assailants, not knowing of his departure, apparently kept shooting until they ran out of ammunition.

Bill, a candidate for Carson Wells' county judge seat, was making campaign stops along the county's back roads when he was attacked. The school board member caught Wells by surprise when he filed for the position, and it was speculated that this was the judge's negative response to his candidacy.

"I should have been with you," Fred Burden declared. "Next time, I'll be along with some of my friends."

Fred paused.

"You're not going to quit are you? This is what the Judge wants and we can't let him have his way. No one has opposed him or his machine in years and it's past due for someone to put him in his place."

"No, I'm not going to quit!" Sanders affirmed. "Wells forced me out of my JP job and I'll never forget it. When you Citation folks convinced me to file for county judge, I knew what I was up against. If it takes a shootout to beat him, so be it!"

Gray Graham, Charley Fitzpatrick and Dr. Clay Stewart—a physician at the junction—had agreed to find a candidate to oppose Wells in his third race for the judgeship. Stewart was a school board member who had been appointed to fill a position left vacant by a member's out-of-state move. He learned quickly about the Wells machine's control of the board and was troubled by it. As a result, he'd become friends with Sanders and Owen Noland, his fellow board members.

Graham, with the support of Fitzpatrick and Stewart, persuaded Sanders to run and had assembled a strong reform organization. They didn't anticipate armed opposition, but they weren't about to back down and knew Bill wouldn't either. However, he would no longer campaign alone.

Burden would make sure of that.

Sanders used the assassination attempt to his advantage, informing audiences that a vote for him was a vote to rid Shawnee County of political outlaws. Word also circulated that Sanders now had an army of his own. On the stump, he emphasized he was appalled that bodyguards were required to insure a free and honest election.

As election day neared, the consensus was that Sanders had made a positive impact. But Fitzpatrick, the campaign manager, urged caution.

"In Shawnee County, the people who cast the votes don't decide an election," he noted. "It's the people who buy and count the votes."

The turnout was huge, and the Sanders team felt good about the two precincts in its region. But a big win locally meant nothing. The Wells organization was a master of dirty tricks and the countywide vote counting indicated it had pulled out all the stops.

County officials announced initially that the Tuesday turnout was so great it feared it would take several days to complete the count. Then, county officials discovered that returns from two northern county precincts had not been counted. When they were, the votes went overwhelming for Wells. Next, it was revealed that several ballot boxes were missing. Some "vandals" had sawed a hole in the counting room floor and absconded with uncounted ballots. The boxes were from precincts believed to favor Sanders.

Late Wednesday, despite all the negativity, it was learned that Sanders was ahead by 243 votes. On Thursday, some so-called corrections saw his lead cut to 131. The next day, an amended precinct return had the race dead even with absentee ballots still to be counted.

Finally, it was announced that Wells had won re-election by 87 votes. Earl Barnes stopped by campaign headquarters to console Sanders and his team.

"You could ask for a recount," he told Bill, "but I think it would be a waste of time. There's no doubt they stole this race, but I don't believe it could be proven. As usual, the absentee balloting went the machine's way.

I'm no longer an election official, but I was told by someone in the know that an extra 200 votes went to Wells when one precinct official changed a seven to a nine. A 795 total for Wells became 995."

"Well, if there's a bright side, Bill remains a school board member and we've gained an ally in Dr. Stewart," Gray commented. "That at least gives us a one-vote margin on board decisions."

"But we still have Jack Nixon to contend with," Owen Noland pointed out. "It'll take another tough campaign to win his seat. Somehow, we've got to find a way to get all our votes to count."

"Or, to keep the machine's vote from counting," Barnes noted. "The only sure way to do that is to get rid of Wells. We came close this time, but we'll survive to fight another day."

Fred Burden left without a word.

Wells and his group had organized a victory party down at Brushy Fork. It began at midday and was still going strong as midnight approached. The Judge was feeling the effects of too much booze and realized it was time to clear his head and call it a night. He relieved himself, ordered some black coffee and drank several cups before he felt sober enough to depart.

Telling his companions to continue partying without him, he made it to his car and began the return trip home. He was driving slowly on the winding road, making sure to avoid any mishaps. As he rounded a curve, he instinctively hit the brakes as another vehicle loomed just ahead.

His headlights illuminated a car that was parked slightly off the road. Its hood was raised and an individual was tinkering with the engine. There was very little room to pass and Wells pulled to a full stop. The man with the stalled vehicle closed the hood and walked toward the Wells car. A cap rested low on his forehead and he carried what appeared to be a tool in his hand.

The judge cranked down his window and called to him.

"I see you're having some trouble. Anything I can do to help?"

The person walked to the open window and peered inside.

"Are you Judge Wells?" he asked.

"I am and how can I be of assistance?"

"By just saying goodbye."

The tool was a pistol. It was pressed against the Judge's temple and fired.

CHAPTER TWENTY-SIX

REVERSAL

A worried Jack Nixon tried to insert his office key into the door lock, but the effort failed. Instead, the motion forced the portal to partly open.

Perspiration beaded across Nixon's brow. He never failed to lock the door when he left his office. Someone had intruded, and the intruder might still be inside.

The murder of Judge Wells had unnerved members of the Shawnee County political machine. Their maneuver to do in Bill Sanders had failed and the opposition had retaliated with a violent act of its own. The machine had stolen the county judge race and had won the battle. But, with the assassination of Wells, the war was on the cusp of being lost.

A school board candidate had been defeated, the machine's candidate for state representative failed to win the Citation precincts, Vito Rossi had been killed, and now the county's long-time leader had been eliminated. What and who was next?

Nixon used his foot to push open the door. It was dark inside, but the odor of tobacco smoke and the glow from a cigar revealed a presence.

"Who's there?" Jack gulped.

"Turn on the lights," he was ordered.

Nixon ran his hand along the wall and punched on the overhead light. The Brushy Fork police chief was seated at Jack's desk. His pistol lay on top and within easy reach.

Nathan Sherman had been the enforcement officer at Bushy Fork for several years. He had been appointed and placed there by Judge Wells, who had been in control of the mine and its lawless community for a decade. Sherman had a shady past, as did his entire staff. The mine manager and his crew also were hand picked by Wells, and the company mined enough coal to keep the operation in the black. But its primary role was machine enforcement and to do the bidding of the county judge.

"What's this about, Nathan?" Nixon asked, expressing his relief in seeing an ally. "And, how did you get in here?"

"It's brass tacks time," the chief replied, placing his hands on the desktop as he pushed to his feet. His side was still stiff from the shootout initiated by Boyd Palmer. His broken nose had healed, but had a slight list to the left.

"As to your second question, I picked the lock," Sherman said. "Come here and sit down. You'll be more comfortable behind your desk and I want you to be comfortable. We're going to discuss the future, and I want your full attention and some straight answers."

The chief shoved his revolver into his waistband, locked the door and settled into a chair facing Nixon. The weapon bothered Jack. It was a bad omen.

"We seem to be on a losing streak," Sherman began. "I've put up with too much inefficiency. First, it was that upstart Palmer kid. He attacked me, shot up my Brushy Fork staff and got away without a scratch. I got no help from you or the machine, but I'll take care of Palmer myself. Nobody invades my place and gets away with it.

"Then, there was the loss of Vito Rossi. He was one hell of a killing machine. And, the last straw was the murder of the judge. I was led to believe the Citation people wouldn't fight back. But, they did, and now our backs are against the wall."

Nixon raised his hands in surrender.

"Okay, but so what? Why are you telling me this? Like you, I was just following the judge's orders."

Sherman placed his arms on the desk and glared at Nixon.

"You were the judge's right hand man. I expected the two of you to keep us on the right path, but you didn't. Now that he's gone, you're in charge."

"Not so," Jack replied. "An interim county judge will have to be appointed and he'll serve until the next election. He'll be the one in charge, not me."

"And who will that be?" Sherman growled. "One of our men or someone sympathetic to that Citation bunch?"

Nixon didn't like the direction of the conversation.

"As I understand it, the circuit judge will make the appointment," he explained. "We won't have a say in it."

The chief lurched to his feet.

"Then you're saying we've lost control!"

Jack's mouth was dry and he licked his lips.

"No, not at all, Nathan. This is just a temporary setback. We couldn't anticipate the attack on Judge Wells, but we'll get our people back on board. We won't be taken down by a two-bit Citation School crowd. We're too big to fail."

Sherman slammed his fists on the desk.

"Too big, hell! We've already failed too many times! I've had it, Jack! I'm getting out and I'm taking my crew with me! I want my share of the war chest and I want it now!"

Nixon took a deep breath. This was no time to lose control. If Sherman and his henchmen left, the machine would be in big trouble. If he paid off the chief, others would want their share and soon the cupboard would be bare. He had to convince Sherman to accept a token payment with the promise of more to come. Or, better yet, what if Nathan could be eliminated and tied to the attacks against Gray Graham and Bill Sanders.

"Tell you what, Nathan," Nixon smiled. "You're right. You've earned your keep and if you want to call it quits, I understand. It'll be tough to go on without you, but we'll get through this.

"Now, as to your share. I don't have all the funds here, but what if I give you something to tide you over and provide the balance in the next few days?"

Sherman was hesitant, but willing to hear more.

"How much now?" he asked.

"How about five thousand?" Nixon suggested.

"I figure I'm owed twenty thousand."

Jack nodded.

"I think that's fair," he said. "Now, don't get hyper on me. I'm going to reach in the bottom drawer and pull out a sack. I think there's at least five thousand in there. Dump the cash on the desk and count it. Okay?"

Nixon placed the sack on the desktop and watched as Sherman extracted the cash and began to count. Jack moved as if to close the drawer, but, instead, grasped a pistol in the rear of the receptacle. He straightened quickly and fired point blank into Sherman's chest.

Hurriedly, he pulled the weapon from Nathan's waistband and fired it into the wall past where he'd been seated. He waited until someone pounded on the door. He mussed his hair and ripped open his shirt, then unlocked the entryway.

"He tried to rob and kill me!" Nixon cried, dropping his weapon to the floor. "Call the police!"

Jack stumbled over to a chair and buried his face in his hands. He effectively portrayed the distraught victim who was forced to defend himself.

Raising his head slowly, he peered at Sherman's body and the individuals kneeling over him.

"Is he dead?

One of the building's office workers glanced at Nixon and nodded. Jack pressed fingers to his forehead and stared at the floor. He feigned anguish as he awaited arrival of the junction police.

Officer Chester Davis paused at the door, taking in the crime scene. He glanced at Nixon, who caught his eye with a steely-eyed glare that spoke volumes. Jack had buttered the officer's bread often with machine money, and Chester knew immediately the role he was to play.

Davis ordered the body removed and asked if anyone had witnessed the event. With no response, he pulled a chair in front of Nixon and asked what had happened.

Jack explained that Nathan Sherman had broken into his office and had awaited his arrival.

"He demanded money and said he was planning to leave town. He was employed by Judge Carson Wells as police chief at Brushy Fork Mine and stated that he feared for his own safety since the judge's assassination.

"I explained that I knew Judge Wells and understood he was part owner of the mine, but knew nothing about his payroll nor his employees. Mr. Sherman became violent and threatened to kill me if I didn't come up with some cash.

"All I had were some proceeds from a fundraiser for our county school libraries. He had a pistol on me and I feared for my life, so I gave him a bank deposit sack with the funds. In the drawer, I noticed the weapon I carried sometimes when I made bank deposits. While he was counting the money, I grabbed the gun and ducked behind the desk. He shot at me and I shot back."

Officer Davis took notes while Nixon was speaking. He stood, shoved the notebook into a pocket and addressed the crowd.

"Let's break it up, folks. This is an unfortunate incident and a clear case of self-defense. Mr. Nixon you're free to go, and we'll be in touch should we have any other questions."

The onlookers were ushered out, and Davis stood with Nixon as Jack locked the office door.

"Well done, Chester. Wrap this up and keep the lid on things. I'll have an envelope for you."

Nixon watched as Davis departed.

'Maybe Nathan Sherman was right,' he thought. 'Our backs are against the wall and maybe it's time to call it quits. Nothing lasts forever.'

CHAPTER TWENTY-SEVEN

AMELIA

"Gray, I believe you know Amelia McIntyre. She's in one of your history classes."

Martha posed the question to her husband as they were finishing their evening meal. Things were quieting down after the shooting at Jack Nixon's office.

"Amelia? Amelia? No, but I know a girl named McIntyre. There's an Amy McIntyre in my world history class that focuses on social issues."

"That's her," Martha said. "I called on her when I substituted in an English class several months ago. I found out later that most people call her Amy."

"She's that little blonde girl who's so extremely shy," Gray said. "What about her?"

Martha had been called on recently to substitute again for Donna Sue McIntosh, one of the Citation school's English teachers who was experiencing a difficult pregnancy. Martha had conducted the writing class for several weeks and had come to know the students fairly well. Amelia, or Amy, was one youngster who intrigued her.

"Amelia must have been impressed by a discussion your class had concerning the necessities of life," Martha explained. "She wrote a paper about it that was outstanding. I want you to read it."

Later that evening, Martha searched through her class materials, found the paper and gave it to Gray. Just before bedtime, he began to read.

I've lived in Shawnee County all of my life. The first time I ever visited a big city was when my uncle, my mother's brother, died. He lived in Huntington. I also had an aunt, my mother's sister, who lived there.

Aunt Cecilia sent us money so we could come to the funeral on the train. I'm the oldest child in my family and my two brothers and a sister are too young for such a trip. So, I went with my mother.

It was a sad time. Everyone loved my uncle, and there was a lot of crying and hugging. When we left to come home, Aunt Cecilia was crying when she hugged us as we got on the train. She told me she was so sorry for me having to grow up in a coal camp and have such a hard life. She said I'd never have the opportunity for better things.

I asked my mother what Aunt Cecilia meant. She said not to be worried about it, that her sister was just upset about my uncle's death. But, I thought a lot about it. I just didn't understand it.

Mr. Graham talked in class one day about the necessities of life. He said if we had the three necessities—food, clothing and shelter—those were the basics for living. If we had that, we could build on it, do good things and become better people. We talked about it in class and I heard my classmates talk about the good things their families were doing. And it seemed those things were happening because, like Mr. Graham said, they were building on the basics for a better life.

I think Aunt Cecilia is wrong. I don't have a hard life. I have a good one. My parents love me and so do my brothers and sister. My daddy works hard, but he gives us the necessities of life and we work together as a family. That's good, and it's fun.

One day after class, I got enough courage to talk with Mr. Graham. I told him I wanted to be a writer some day, but I didn't know if that was a good thing to do. It might not give me food, clothing and shelter.

He said I already had that and now was the time to build on it. He said I could be anything I wanted if I were willing to keep working for it. He said it might be hard, but not to give up. He said I came from a good family, that I was smart and he knew that a lot of good things were going to happen for me. He said just to follow my dream, become a good writer and apply myself. That will earn you the necessities of life, he said, and that I would have a life I'd enjoy and be a productive member of society.

He said he was confident that I would make my family, my friends and my teachers proud. He said that included him. And, he couldn't wait to read all the good things I'd write about.

I feel good about things. I know I'm beginning to build a good future. Maybe I can even convince Aunt Cecilia.

Gray wiped his eyes and cleared his throat just before his wife came to check on him.

"Aren't you coming to bed? It's getting late."

"Sit down for a minute," he said. "Wow! That's quite a paper. This girl is really something."

Martha nodded in agreement.

"What do you know about her?" she asked. "She's only fourteen and so shy that I'm amazed she would open up to you."

"I've met her father, but, it's like my relationship with so many of the miners. I don't know him very well. I've seen his wife at some of our school functions and she's very quiet and probably shy like Amy. Mac McLeod says Sam McIntyre is a hard worker and is devoted to his family. He said if there was ever anyone to put his family first, McIntyre would head the list."

"I wish I'd heard your lecture about the necessities of life," Martha remarked. "It must have been one of your better teaching days."

"It was an unusual day," Gray said. "You know what I mean. You're all prepared to follow a lesson plan that you've delivered before, and, all of a sudden, someone asks a question or something else happens to put things in a different direction. Somehow, necessities struck a nerve and I'll always remember that day as the time I got through to Jimmy Dan. It was one of my proudest moments."

Gray smiled as he reminisced.

"I felt I'd done something that made a difference."

Martha pulled Gray to his feet and kissed him.

"You did. And that lesson and the encouragement you provided Amelia gave her some shining moments."

She hooked her arm around that of Gray and led him to bed.

"As we say in Eastern Kentucky, 'You done good,' husband."

CHAPTER TWENTY-EIGHT

THE DANCE

Eileen's dress was extraordinary.

It was royal blue, mid-length and emphasized her slim waist and narrow hips. She had made it herself in the chic style of the thirties. Martha was impressed.

"It's beautiful, Eileen!" she gushed. "You'll be turning a lot of heads!"

Martha then paused and asked Eileen to slowly twirl.

"Hmmm, it needs one thing," she mused. "I'll be right back."

She returned with some pearl earrings and a matching bracelet. They were the perfect accessories. Taking Eileen's hand, she led her into the hallway.

"Let's go show Gray."

Cracking open the door to the apartment, she saw her husband pouring over the newspaper. Martha stepped inside and asked Gray to close his eyes.

"Get ready for a surprise," she smiled, leading Eileen to stand before him. "Okay, open your eyes!"

Gray blinked and smiled.

"Eileen, you're beautiful! If I weren't married, I'd be after you in a minute!"

Martha feigned anger and threw a pillow, which he caught. Gray stood, took Eileen's hand and spun her.

"So, that's the dress Martha was telling me about. I didn't know you were an expert seamstress in addition to your other talents. This must be for a special occasion."

"Oh, yes!" Eileen gushed. "Boyd Palmer is taking me to a dance in Huntington! It's a dance marathon!"

The Grahams looked at one another in surprise.

"A dance marathon!" Martha cried. "Do you know what you're getting into?"

"It's going to be great fun," Eileen said. "I'm a good dancer, and I think Boyd and I can win some prizes. Boyd says all prizes are paid in cash and that we could win as much as $1,000 if we finish in first place. But, even if we don't, we still could win several hundred dollars. Boyd said he heard of someone getting $100 just for finishing in fifth place."

"Eileen, a dance marathon is all about endurance, not how good a dancer you are," Gray explained. "Winners of these events have to dance constantly for 24 hours or more. This means no sleep, no rest and a lot of physical pain and discomfort. Don't believe it's just going to be fun."

Martha nodded in agreement.

"I remember reading about a dance marathon where a man died. He was on his feet for days and collapsed from exhaustion. He died on the dance floor."

Eileen interrupted.

"That won't happen to us," she declared. "Boyd says we'll get fifteen minute breaks every hour and we'll be served meals and snacks. We'll even have time to visit the bathroom. And, a nurse is always on duty and a doctor is on call should anything serious occur. You guys are looking at the bad things that could happen."

"So, what are the good things?" Martha asked.

"Well, the main thing is that it'll be fun. And, even if we don't win the big prizes, Boyd says there's other money to be made. He said he knows of one couple who won prize money in a talent show during a marathon. And, for good dancers like us, people throw money on the floor if you're one of their favorites.

"Boyd said some couples win sponsorships from local businesses and, if people really like you, he's heard that you can get cash by selling autographs and getting your picture taken."

Eileen extended her arms and twirled again.

"I'm glad you like the dress. I just hope Boyd will."

"That's the least of your worries," Gray grinned. "He'll have a movie queen on his arm. Hedy Lamarr would have a jealous fit if she were to see you."

Eileen kissed Gray on the cheek and hugged Martha.

"We'll drive to Huntington Friday night and come back Sunday evening," she explained. "Wish us luck!"

Eileen danced her way out the door as the Grahams waved goodbye.

"Gray, I love that girl," Martha sighed. "She's like the younger sister I never had. I'll worry about her the whole time she's gone. I wish she weren't going, particularly with Boyd Palmer. I really don't trust him."

Graham embraced his wife and gave her a lingering kiss.

"You're really something," he said. "Living with me is enough of a challenge and you have your hands full with Jack and teaching part time. And, now, you're mothering Eileen. Ease up, she'll be all right."

Martha rested her head on Gray's shoulder.

"I hope you're right. But, she's going to be with Boyd non-stop for a full weekend. He'll have his hands all over her and I just hope the worst won't happen. She's too trusting, and I think she's in love with him. It's not a pretty picture."

But when Boyd and Eileen hit the dance floor, it was a pretty picture. It turned out that both had great rhythm, possessed tremendous footwork and demonstrated lots of energy. And, they were versatile. They not only knew the currently popular dances, but were adept at those of the Roaring Twenties.

They began the marathon with a foxtrot, followed by a waltz and the audience took notice. Dance marathons usually attracted sizeable crowds at twenty-five cents a pop, but the onlookers were used to seeing a slow shuffle as the performers saved their energy for the long haul.

Boyd asked that the music be turned up several notches and he and Eileen jumped into a spirited version of the Charleston. Other dancers moved to the sidelines as the Citation duo took center stage.

"How can they do that?" one man inquired. "They better conserve their energy."

"Who cares!" his wife cried as applause filled the oversized ballroom. "They're great!"

Boyd and Eileen warmed to the response and the musicians adapted to the speed and rhythm of their movements. They returned to a slow Foxtrot to catch their breath then sped into the Black Bottom. Suddenly, a marathon had been transformed into a dazzling floor show.

The first fifteen-minute break was called and the stars of the show were greeted with great applause and substantial rewards. Boyd was handed a hat filled with bills and change, and Eileen was given a purse with more of the same. The crowd called for more as dancing resumed.

The Foxtrot became an energy-saving staple, but the audience called for more fast-paced dances. The Jive, the Lindy Hop and the Big Apple were added during the second hour, but it drove Boyd and Eileen to near exhaustion. They slumped into chairs at the second break while others retreated to a rest area.

They were too tired to continue.

CHAPTER TWENTY-NINE

THE REWARDS

A master of ceremonies stepped to the dance floor with a microphone and raised his hands for quiet.

"As you know, ladies and gentlemen, it is a tradition for dance marathons to award cash prizes to particularly talented performers. I think you will agree that one of our couples certainly qualifies for ample praise and accolades."

The applause was deafening.

"The best floor show I've ever seen!" one person yelled.

"This is better than going to the picture show!" another cried.

The MC held up his hands for quiet and extracted three envelopes from a pocket.

"This prize money is for the best dancing couple of the morning. Please give a big hand to Boyd Palmer and Eileen Branscomb."

They were given their prize and told to remain with the MC.

"Also, we have a reward for the most handsome couple," he announced. "And we know who that is. Congratulations again Boyd and Eileen!"

As they turned to leave, the MC grasped Eileen's arm.

"Don't leave just yet, Miss Branscomb," he broadcast. "This next prize is for the most beautiful dancer."

He was unable to finish the presentation as the applause and whistles drowned him out. Eileen accepted the award along with a kiss from the MC before the crowd rushed onto the floor. With the assistance of some attendants, the throng was ushered to the sidelines as marathoners returned. Eileen and Boyd were too exhausted to join them.

"My name is Denver Logan," one enthusiast said as he shook Palmer's hand. "Here's my card. I'm the proprietor of Logan's Furniture here in Huntington and I want to hire you and your partner to participate in a huge sale I'm planning."

"But we don't know anything about selling furniture," Boyd said.

"You don't need to," Logan declared. "I want you to perform and draw a crowd. I'll do the selling."

Logan pushed a $20 bill into Palmer's hand.

"There's more of that to come. Let's stay in touch."

One of the attendants brought Boyd and Eileen some refreshments and explained there was more food and drink in the rest area.

"Since you don't plan to continue, feel free to relax and get some rest," he said.

The rest area was an adjoining room that was used by the marathoners at break time. Cots also were available for those wishing to grab a few minutes of sleep. Fifteen-minute breaks didn't allow much time for rest, but even a few minutes were precious as the hours lengthened.

Boyd collapsed on one cot and Eileen took another.

"Oh-h-h," she groaned. "My feet and legs will never be the same!"

Eileen sat on the edge of the cot and rubbed her feet. She'd worn her most comfortable shoes, but even the best footwear couldn't support hours of hectic non-stop dancing.

Boyd lay with his hands behind his head. His thoughts were of the prize money and the things it could buy. He'd give Eileen her share, but he could do all kinds of fun things with his portion. They'd made out like bandits, and the offer from the furniture baron promised a lot more. Several people even paid for their autographs.

Palmer was too excited to rest. He spied containers with food, iced tea and coffee on a nearby table and stood to partake. He made himself a sandwich and poured a glass of tea before returning to his cot.

"How about something to eat?" he called to Eileen.

"I don't think so," she groaned. "Is there any coffee?"

"Sure, I'll bring you some," he said.

The coffee in the percolator was still hot and Palmer filled a nearby mug. He placed it on a tray with some biscuits and marmalade and dragged a table and chair to Eileen's cot. He'd added small cream and sugar pitchers to the tray.

Eileen added a spoonful of sugar and a touch of cream to the drink and took several sips before speaking.

"You're quite a dancer, Boyd," she smiled. "How did you know all those dances from the twenties?"

"I've led an interesting life," he grinned. "I took the train to Chicago with my dad one summer and we took in the best night spots. I guess I shouldn't tell this, but we spent some time at a former speakeasy and Dad invited one of the dancers to our table. We talked and drank and, after her last performance, she came back and we talked and drank some more.

"I told her what a great dancer she was and, at closing time, she invited me to learn a few steps. We did it without music, but she showed me the fundamentals. She said I was a natural. With her instruction and viewing other dancers later on, I guess I just took to it. How about you?"

"My parents love to dance," Eileen said. "On Saturday night they'd roll up the rug, turn on the radio and dance to all the big band music. When my sister and I were old enough they'd let us join in. There wasn't a dance my folks didn't like and they taught them all to Susan and me.

"But I've never danced like we did today. When I heard all the applause I got carried away. I must have danced the last hour on adrenalin. I don't think my feet and legs will ever be the same."

"Are you still hurting?"

"Yes, and I can't get comfortable sitting or lying down."

"Let me rub your feet," Boyd said. "That may help you relax."

She instructed Boyd to turn away so she could remove her stockings. She smoothed her dress as she lay on the cot and extended her feet. Boyd began messaging, moving from one foot to the other.

"Oh, Boyd," she called. "That feels great. Don't stop."

Palmer didn't. He gradually moved to the calves of her legs and Eileen closed her eyes in ecstasy. Boyd, she decided, had magic hands and a technique that was like a healing caress. But her eyes blinked open when his hands swept over her thighs.

"What are you doing!" she asked in alarm as she pushed down her skirt.

"Sh-h-h," Boyd soothed. "Just relax. No one else is here. I'm just trying to help."

Eileen started to sit up, but Boyd gently pushed her down as his lips found hers. His kiss was long and passionate and aroused a primal need. She embraced him and returned his kiss, pulling him closer. Boyd eased a hand under her dress and pulled down her panties.

She proved to be willing and able.

CHAPTER THIRTY

FRED

Earl Barnes opened a drawer and sat a bottle of bourbon whiskey atop the desk. He poured a shot into Gray Graham's coffee cup, then added a shot for himself.

Gray looked up, a question in his eyes.

"What's this?" he asked.

"A little pick-me-up," the attorney replied. "I think we both can use it. We've been through a lot together."

Graham had stopped by Barnes' law office to discuss the area's political future and how the Citation school might be affected. This was in view of Carson Wells death and the anticipated downfall of his political machine.

Gray shook his head and chuckled.

"It's been amazing. All the shootings, the elections, my problems with Judge Wells, his murder, and now we're awaiting the appointment of an interim county judge. What's next?"

Barnes took a sip from his cup and grinned.

"Good times—that's what's next. Whoever the next interim judge is, I think we can expect a big improvement for Shawnee County. Unofficially, I know some of the potential candidates under consideration and they're all good men. Relax and don't start second-guessing."

"Maybe I'm a worrywart, Earl, but I don't believe things happen without a reason. Vito Rossi was hired to take me out along with other school supporters. But all of a sudden, he disappeared. We had some really surprising school board victories against a political machine with expertise in buying votes and rearranging ballot boxes. Then, we lost the county judge race, but, again, out of the blue, Judge Wells was murdered.

That made it possible to end a corrupt political machine."

"So, what's your point?"

"Who or what made all this happen? What's the common denominator?"

"Knowing you, I'll wager you've found one."

Graham gazed at Barnes before responding.

"Fred Burden," he said.

Earl took a deep breath and leaned back in his chair.

"Interesting," he replied.

"You know the story about Fred taking the library funds and losing it in a pool game," Gray continued. "He then came to me, confessed, and said he owed me a big debt because of what my father had done for his dad where a potential shooting was concerned. He said that if I ever got in a bind, I could count on him.

"From that point on, Fred was always there when we had a problem. Did he dispose of Rossi and Judge Wells? Did he do some undercover work where the elections were concerned? I can't prove anything. But I really believe Fred was a factor."

Barnes righted his chair and placed his forearms on the desk. He paused in thought before speaking.

"How much do you know about Fred?"

"Not a lot," Graham said.

"Well," the attorney replied, "I don't know how this may tie in with your thinking, but Fred comes from a family with a history of righting wrongs. And, they don't waste time doing it.

"What do you know about the assassination of William Goebel?"

"That's another bloody incident in Kentucky history," Gray remarked. "Goebel is the only state governor in the United States to be assassinated while in office. That happened in Frankfort in 1900 as I recall, and he only served about four days before he died. But how's that significant where Fred and his family are concerned?"

"It's been said that the Burdens were involved," Earl related. "It fact, the story is that it was one of Burdens who shot Goebel."

"My gosh, could that be true?"

Barnes pursed his lips and shook his head.

"I have no idea, but it's something to think about. The identity of Goebel's assassin is still unknown."

It was after three o'clock and, with the school day ended, Gray made his rounds to make sure everything was shipshape. The light still was on in Bernice Burden's classroom, and he stopped to take a look. Bernice was putting away some paperwork and Fred was seated nearby, waiting to take his wife home.

"You're working late, Bernice," Graham smiled, then turned to her husband. "Take her home, Fred. You and I know we can't pay her overtime."

Burden waved to the principal.

"And you and I know she wouldn't take it if you gave it to her. She's all about dedication and doing things right."

Gray sat on the edge of a student desk, Fred's comment having struck a chord.

"That's something you two have in common, which brings up something else. I was a history and political science major in college and I've taught a number of Kentucky history classes. One of my interests concerning the state's past is the assassination of William Goebel. I've heard all sorts of stories about that incident and I've been told your family has some first-hand information. I'd like to talk with you about it when you have some time."

Burden sat up straight, and he and Bernice exchanged a glance.

"What have you heard?" he asked.

"Just that some of your family were in Frankfort when it happened. I'd sure like to hear an eyewitness account."

Fred's face had turned grim.

"That happened before I was born. I can't give an eyewitness account."

"Oh, I know that Fred and I don't mean to pry. I just thought you might have a family story about the event. That's all."

An uncomfortable silence prevailed.

"Oh, forget it Fred," Gray said. "I've touched on something you're not comfortable with and I apologize if I'm out of line. I hope you know how grateful I am for your support and friendship. You've stood by me during some tough times here and I'll forever be in your debt."

Graham stood, clapped his hands and smiled.

"Come on, let's go home. Tomorrow's another day!"

The Burdens never moved and Fred stared intently at Gray.

"I like you, Graham," Fred said, breaking the uncomfortable silence.

"You stand up for what you believe and you've always been fair with me. If you really want to know something about the Goebel shooting I'll tell you. But, not here. Come by our house Saturday and we'll talk."

CHAPTER THIRTY-ONE

THE STORY

It was early Saturday afternoon when Gray Graham approached the Burden residence. He reached the front door, but before he could knock it was opened.

"I've been expecting you," Fred said, ushering Graham inside.

They sat in a small living room and Burden got straight to the point.

"You want to know about the shooting of William Goebel," Fred announced. "But first, tell me what you know."

"Well, it's on record that the 1899 gubernatorial election was a very heated event," Gray began. "Goebel, a Democrat, was opposed by Republican William Taylor and, with all the ballots counted, Taylor won by a little more than 2,000 votes.

"Democrats in the General Assembly said there were voting irregularities in some counties and created a committee to investigate voter fraud. The Board of Elections, however, ruled that the disputed ballots should count, stating they had no legal power to reverse official county results. The Kentucky Constitution, however, gave the power to review the election to the General Assembly, and the heavily Democratic Assembly invalidated enough Republican votes to give the election to Goebel. Needless to say, the Republicans were incensed."

Burden smiled and nodded to Graham.

"You know your history. Go on."

"Pending a final decision, Taylor served as governor, but the Republicans saw the writing on the wall. Goebel was going to be declared the winner, and apparently there was a surge of armed citizens from

Republican Eastern Kentucky into Frankfort. They were determined to keep Goebel and the Democrats from stealing the election."

Fred raised his hand to interrupt.

"Everyone knew they were armed," he said, "because they were wearing their guns openly. That was to avoid arrest for carrying a concealed weapon."

"And that added to the tensions that some thought might provoke a civil war," Gray added.

"That leads us to the shooting of Goebel," Fred noted. "What do you know about that?"

"Goebel, as I recall, was a state senator at the time and was well aware there was a rumored assassination plot against him," Gray said. "He apparently had some bodyguards, and they were with him as he was walking to the state capitol. That would have been the morning of January 30 and when his assassin, or assassins, opened fire on him.

"The reports are fuzzy at this point, but apparently five or six shots were fired and one hit Goebel in the chest. The day after he was shot, Goebel was sworn in as governor. But four days later he died."

Graham sat back and looked at Burden.

"Well, Fred, how did I do? That's what I know. Tell me how this jibes with your family's story."

Bernice brought in some coffee and took a chair.

"I know what Fred's going to tell, but I want to hear it again. Hope you don't mind if I join you."

"Not at all, Bernice," Gray said. "Go ahead, Fred."

Burden looked down, gathering his thoughts.

"My Uncle Morton Burden was my dad's older brother. What I'm going to tell you is what Mort told the family about the shooting. He was there. What you said about a group from Eastern Kentucky going to Frankfort is true. Mort was in that group and all of them were mad as hell about their votes for Taylor not being validated. They were convinced that Goebel and his supporters were going to steal the election.

"One thing my family despises is a thief or a group of thieves. We have a history of doing whatever is necessary to go after them and exact justice. This may surprise you, as you know I took the school's library funds and lost them playing pool. If you hadn't recovered them, I would have. When I get drunk I do stupid things, and taking that money was one of the worst. I've tried to make up for it by supporting you in every way I can."

Bernice interrupted.

"Get back on the subject, Fred. We already know you can do some stupid things."

"Yeah, yeah, okay. Where was I? Oh, I was telling about Mort and his trip to Frankfort. Well, Mort and the group he was with weren't going to stand for Goebel's people to steal the election. They were really spoiling for a fight and the police and city officials were doing everything they could to keep the peace. Part of Mort's group were fed up with all the political bickering and were all for 'shooting Boss Bill and all his outlaws.'

"Just about everyone had a pistol, but it was common knowledge that no one could get close enough with a pistol to shoot someone without being caught. Apparently, that's when someone came up with the idea of using a rifle.

"Then, according to Mort, a plan was developed for taking out Goebel. The shooting was to take place from a building near the capitol."

"That would have been the secretary of state's office," Gray injected. "It was in the annex left of the capitol."

"So what," an aggravated Fred replied. "Don't interrupt me, Graham, I'm telling the story."

"Sorry, go on."

"As I was saying, the plan called for the shot to be taken from a window on the first floor. The shooter then would take the weapon and shove it through the transom of a nearby office. Someone inside the office would take the rifle to another window, where a wagon filled with hay would be located. The rifle would be dropped into the wagon and the driver would leave with it.

"Again, according to Mort, there was so much confusion following the shooting that the rifle was never dropped off in the wagon. But the shot was on target. Goebel took it in the chest. It was a fatal blow and he never recovered."

Burden paused and there was a moment of quiet. Graham absorbed what Fred had reported before he spoke.

"My research indicated that the bullet Goebel took was .38 caliber, passed through his body and was imbedded in a tree. From the angle of the body and the bullet in the tree, the consensus was that the shot probably was fired from the secretary of state building. That agrees with what you said, Fred.

"Also, five who were charged with the shooting went to trial. Two were acquitted, and the three others eventually were pardoned by subsequent governors. The identity of the assassin never was discovered."

Burden took a sip of coffee and frowned.

"Bernice, I can't drink this—it's cold."

"That's because you're such a windbag," she countered.

"Fred, that's quite a story," Gray commented. "But I can't help but wonder if your Uncle Mort knew who fired the fatal shot. He never said?"

"Nope."

With that, Burden stood and left the room. A puzzled Graham looked at Bernice. She shrugged her shoulders.

"He'll be back," she said.

A few moments later Fred returned with a bundle in his hands. It was an elongated item wrapped in a blanket. He unfolded the covering and held up the object.

"This is the weapon," he said.

Gray took the rifle and examined it before returning it to Fred. They stared at each other, but neither spoke.

As he departed, a myriad of thoughts ran through Graham's mind. Maybe the murders in Shawnee County simply were following a pattern of righting wrongs and disposing of corruption. And maybe it began nearly four decades ago in Frankfort.

CHAPTER THIRTY-TWO

BASEBALL

Charley Fitzpatrick laid the uniform on Gray Graham's desk.

"What's this?" Gray asked.

"It's your baseball uniform. We're a man short and need you to play Sunday."

"You've got to be kidding," Graham snorted. "I played last season when I had time, but with graduate school and this job I can't do it anymore. Sorry, Charley, but you'll have to find someone else."

Coalfield baseball had become a big thing in Southern Appalachia, but only recently in Southeastern Kentucky. A four-team league had been formed three years earlier and had expanded to six teams the past season. Each ball club was sponsored by its coal company. The mining firms saw the sport as a way to bring their communities together and provide a recreational outlet for their hard-working miners.

Citation was the last league holdout. All company employees were eligible to participate, and a signed petition by a majority of male personnel requesting sponsorship caused Selkirk officials to capitulate.

As such, Selkirk agreed to provide a playing field, uniforms and appropriate equipment. A grandstand and scoreboard were also included. Games were played on Sunday afternoons.

The Citation team struggled its first season. The ball field was located in one of the few remaining flat land areas. At best, it was rugged with a rocky surface that was pitted with holes. And, the opposition was formidable. Several teams had gone all out to win, hiring minor league players for "above ground" jobs. Brushy Fork, Citation's next opponent, was one of those.

"Come on, Gray, where's your community spirit?" Charley, the team player-manager, pleaded. "We can't be beaten by Brushy Fork again. They won every game against us last season and have lorded it over us ever since. We need you in the outfield."

Gray vehemently shook his head.

"Absolutely not! I nearly broke my legs last season tripping over stones and stepping into holes."

"It won't happen again," Charley emphasized. "Mac McLeod has the field raked and grass cut on a regular basis. And, the rocks have been removed and the holes have been filled."

"Where did he get the extra soil to fill the holes?"

Fitzpatrick shuffled his feet and gazed at the floor.

"He couldn't find enough dirt. He had to fill them with cinders.

"But," Charley continued, "they were pounded out and smoothed over. If you didn't know they were cinders you couldn't tell the difference.

"Look, Gray, we need your bat. As far as I'm concerned, you can sleep in left field as long as you're available to hit. Come on. How about it?"

Gray's father had been a semi-pro baseball legend in Shawnee County. He would either hit a home run or strike out swinging. His son was his clone.

"Okay, Charley," Graham reluctantly agreed. "We don't need more bragging rights from Brushy Fork."

As an afterthought he raised another question.

"Who's pitching?"

"Who else?" Fitzpatrick responded. "Bull Elliott."

Graham groaned.

"Charley, I think the world of Bull, but as a pitcher he's more of a thrower."

"Yeah, but a hard thrower," Fitzpatrick pointed out. "He can throw a straight ball through a barn door."

That was a fact. When team tryouts were conducted that first season, a practice session was conducted at a nearby farm where an ancient barn was used as back stop. When asked to throw a high hard one, Bull sailed one that splintered a piece of barn siding and ricocheted off an inside wall. And, unfortunately, Bull was Citation's primary baseball weapon.

William (Bull) Elliott, Citation's dynamite specialist, was the father of William Garrett (Little Bull) Elliott. He and his son could charm the socks off most anyone, but could be massive forces when angered.

"Now don't second-guess Bull's ability," Charley cautioned. "I'll wager he has a fastball that would rival the Big Train."

The Big Train was Walter Johnson, the fabled major league pitcher who had a virtually unhittable fastball.

"Yeah, I know," Gray agreed, "but the difference is that Johnson could control his pitch, but Elliott can't."

"Well, we've never had a batter dig in against Bull," Fitzpatrick emphasized.

"Not if they wanted to live and play another day," Graham smirked.

"This year Bull has added a drop pitch," Charley revealed. "Along with his straight ball, batters are totally fooled. Brushy Fork won't be able to hit him at all."

"They won't have to," Gray sighed. "He'll hit them first."

Graham stuffed the uniform into his brief case. Sunday afternoon would be interesting.

Bull started game day with unusual control. He struck out the first two batters he faced before hitting the third. He got out of the inning when the next batter grounded weakly to the mound and was thrown out at first.

After the third inning, Elliott went native. His first pitch was ten feet over the catcher's head and the ball stuck in the backstop wire. His next two pitches were in the dirt and were blocked by the catcher. At this point, runners were on first and third and Fitzpatrick called time.

"You're throwing too hard, Bull," he explained. "Take a little off on your pitches. We don't want to walk this batter and load the bases."

But, before the next pitch, the runner on third decided to steal home. That confused Bull. He didn't know if he should let up on the pitch or throw it hard to beat the base runner. It ended up that he threw it hard and beaned the runner as he neared home. The runner was knocked out and fell about six feet from the plate. The ball bounced all the way to Fitzpatrick at shortstop who threw it to the catcher, who, by instinct, tagged out the runner.

The umpire called him out—which he really was—and that ended the inning.

In the next inning, Bull got two strikes on the batter, then threw a high hard one that skipped off the catcher's glove and hit the umpire on the upper part of his facemask. The concussion so addled the ump that he had to leave the game.

Citation finally got two outs. The next batter was a former Cincinnati Reds farmhand with several years of professional experience. He glared at Elliott and purposely dug in. That was a mistake.

Bull put all of his 260 pounds into his next pitch. Walter Johnson would have been proud of its velocity, but not its result. The batter was beaned and fell unconscious. The Bushy Fork players stormed the mound and the Citation team met them head on.

Charley and Gray jumped into the melee and wrestled two of the opposition to the ground. With no umpire to stop it, the battle raged and the crowd joined in, primarily to support Bull. But the burly Elliott needed no help.

He delivered a roundhouse right to the first Brushy Fork player who charged him. He followed by banging the heads together of two others, took a bat from another and laid out a trio of infielders. The slugfest surged into the outfield where, with the help of the crowd, Citation was winning the struggle.

Bull stood in the outfield, his shirt in threads, as the Brushy Fork contingent began a retreat. Then, someone hit Elliott in the face with a baseball. Unable to determine who threw the ball, Bull raced to his bench and withdrew a metal container containing dynamite.

He withdrew a handful of sticks and a box of matches and made his way toward the Brushy Fork vehicles. Charley intercepted and demanded to know what he was doing.

"I'm going to blow those bastards to hell!" he bellowed. "They've picked on us for the last time!"

"You can't do that, Bull!" Charley shouted. "That's murder! You could be sent to prison!"

"Get out of the way, Charley! Those bastards are going to pay!"

Gray and Liam McLeod ran up to form a moving blockade. Mac was waving a rulebook.

"You can't do this, Bull!" he ordered.

"Why not!"

"Because it's against the rules!" Mac said, thumbing through the manual. "It says right here dynamite can't be used in baseball!"

Stunned, Bull stopped with a look of bewilderment.

"Oh!" he said. "I didn't know that."

He returned the contents and laid down the box.

CHAPTER THIRTY-THREE

TURNING POINT

"I'll open with ten," the first player said, throwing $10 into the pot.

"Let's make it fifty," Boyd Palmer responded.

The pot now contained more than $200 in cash along with a substantial amount of scrip. Dealer Fred Burden estimated that the script, worth seventy-five cents on the dollar, boosted the take to nearly $500.

Not to be outdone, player three said, "Let's make it one hundred."

"If you don't mind, how about two hundred," Carl Ramsay suggested, tossing more bills onto the table.

"Too rich for me," one said as he folded. Boyd and another followed suit.

The poker competition at the junction saloon had taken high stakes proportions and only Burden and Ramsay remained. They studied their hands before Fred called for cards.

"I'll stand pat," Ramsay smiled.

"The dealer takes two," Fred stated.

Ramsay was a seasoned poker player and a successful gambler. Burden was on a winning streak and determined to take down the man who had a reputation as being Shawnee County's best at this game of chance.

"What have you got?" Fred asked.

Ramsay spread his four jacks. Burden hesitated, then showed his hand.

"I think a straight flush beats four of a kind," he said, raking in the pot.

Ramsay never changed expression, but unbuttoned his coat revealing a pistol in his waistband. Fred had won the last three rounds.

"I say you've been cheating," Ramsay declared.

"So this is the way it's going to end," Burden remarked, stuffing the winnings into his pockets. "But, I caution you, don't move your hand any closer to that weapon. Mr. Palmer, the gentleman directly across from you, is a friend of mine and he really hates sore losers. You'll notice that he only has one hand on the table. He has the other underneath with a .38 that's pointed at your stomach.

"Now, this is my weapon," he continued, drawing his pistol. "I'd like you and your friends to place your hands on the table. And, do it slowly. Boyd and I are going to leave now and I suggest you remain in your seats. Come after us at your own risk. We'll be waiting outside and we won't hesitate to take you down."

It was like a scene from a western movie. Weapons in hand, they backed out of the room and Fred motioned for them to take cover. Boyd eased over to his roadster and extracted two more handguns. He tossed one to Fred.

"How much longer?" he asked Burden.

"Anytime now," Fred replied. "They'll hit the door all at once with guns blazing. Don't be surprised if there's more than just the ones at our table. I'm guessing that Ramsay will gain some support from inside."

Palmer checked the loads in his pistols.

"If you're right, we better pick our targets carefully. We don't want to run out of ammunition."

As predicted, the door burst open with fire from six men who spread out in front of the building. Fred and Boyd wounded two and retreated into the doorways of nearby structures. Sporadic firing ensued, as each side sought an advantage. Suddenly, Ramsay's group charged and Fred and Boyd were forced to retreat.

It became a running gun battle, with Burden and Palmer fleeing in different directions. That split the opposition, as two followed Fred and the remaining duo raced after Boyd.

The gun battle extended into a residential area and, in the open space, Palmer was an easy target. He staggered as he was hit in the leg, but kept running. Another bullet passed through a shoulder and into a lung as he stumbled toward an apartment building. He supported himself against its wall as he coughed up blood. His legs were turning weak and his vision became blurred, but, with his back to the wall, he turned to face an impending death.

With both pistols in hand, he fired until the weapons were empty. Boyd's body jerked with each bullet he took as his pursuers closed in. He died beneath a window where a youngster inside marveled at the scene.

The young boy was laughing. This was better than a cowboy movie, he rejoiced.

The pounding on the door was incessant. An alarmed Martha Graham rushed to open it and a sobbing Eileen Branscomb fell into her arms. She maneuvered her onto a sofa and embraced Eileen as the young nurse buried her head in Martha's bosom. Eileen's uncontrolled weeping continued despite Martha's attempts to console her.

Finally, Eileen became sufficiently composed to speak.

"Oh, Martha!" she sobbed. "Boyd has been killed!"

Martha was shocked, but continued to hold Eileen.

"Oh my gosh, what happened!"

"He was gambling over at the junction," Eileen cried. "He and Fred Burden were in a card game and Mr. Burden was accused of cheating. It ended up in a gunfight and Boyd was killed. They brought Mr. Burden over to our office and Dr. Bradbury is working on him."

"Is Fred going to die?"

"No," Eileen said, wiping tears from her cheeks. "He has some bad wounds, but Dr. Bradbury says none are life threatening. I was trying to assist, but I was so out of control that one of Mr. Burden's friends took me back to my apartment.

"I just couldn't stay there by myself," she declared. "This is just awful!"

Martha stroked Eileen's cheek and kissed her forehead.

"I know it is," she said. "But you have to pull yourself together. Boyd wouldn't want you to suffer this way."

"He wouldn't care!" Eileen shrieked. "You don't know the half of it!"

Martha pushed her to arms length.

"What are you saying? Of course he would!"

"Martha, I'm pregnant!" she declared. "I told Boyd and he didn't care. He said he wasn't going to be tied down with a wife and a baby. I told him I loved him and wanted to marry him, but he just laughed. He said I should have been more careful.

"I went to see his mother, but Mrs. Palmer was worse than Boyd. She said she wasn't Boyd's mother and was fed up with having to 'clean up after him' and wasn't going to do it anymore. She told me that Mr. Palmer had slept with a woman at Ashland who showed up one day with a baby and gave it to him. She said the woman told him 'it's yours and it's yours to take care of.'

"Mrs. Palmer said her husband persuaded her to accept the child and, reluctantly, she helped to rear him. She said Boyd was wild and always out of control and she regretted having ever been part of his life. She kicked him out when he turned eighteen and told Boyd she never wanted to see him again."

Eileen slumped against the sofa and sighed.

"What am I going to do, Martha? I'm a defiled woman who soon will have an out-of-wedlock child. I can't stay here, but I don't know where to go."

Martha took Eileen's hands.

"Have you told your parents?"

"I don't know how to tell them. This will break their hearts."

"They'll help you, Eileen. I know a girl who went through what you're experiencing. Her parents took her to another town to have the baby, and she returned saying that her husband had died. You could do the same thing and people would accept it. You could start over with a fresh beginning. If you want, I'll be glad to talk to your parents."

Eileen shook her head and stood.

"No, I've got to do this myself. The important thing now is the baby. If my parents will help, I'll give it a good home and a good life."

Martha gave her a hug.

"You're doing the right thing. It won't be easy, and I'll help in any way I can."

Martha placed her hands on Eileen's cheeks and smiled.

"Don't let this get you down. You're going to be a great mother and will love and be loved by a great child. You're going to make all of us proud."

CHAPTER THIRTY-FOUR

DARK HORIZON

"We're on the brink of a second world war and sooner or later this country will be dragged into it," Liam McLeod declared. "If I were you, Gray, I'd be thinking about that."

Graham looked at the mine manager with surprise.

"I'm not sure of your meaning, Mac. Are you asking how I would handle such a situation as a teacher?"

Mac shook his head.

"No, how would you deal with it personally?'

McLeod had asked Graham to meet with him in his office. Gray had guessed it had something to do with the school. He worried that it might involve finances or total transfer of the learning center to the county. An economic problem was foremost among possible difficulties.

"What are you getting at?" he asked.

"You read the newspapers and listen to the radio," Mac stated. "The world news is about Germany and its intentions concerning Poland. Those in the know speculate that Adolf Hitler will invade and take control of that country probably without a shot being fired. When that happens, Great Britain and France won't stand for it and World War II will begin."

Graham chuckled.

"You amaze me, Mac. I never knew you were so knowledgeable about international politics."

"I was called to Pittsburgh last week for a planning session on the future of the coal industry," McLeod explained. "Selkirk called in industry and governmental experts to speculate on what might happen if another world war were to occur. If that should happen, it will have a major affect on the mining and production of coal."

Gray gestured in agreement.

"I believe that's true, but, really, all this is conjecture. I'm sure it also was mentioned in the planning session that America would be reluctant to enter into a world war. This country has had a longstanding reluctance to get involved in European alliances and conflicts. We know that from our study of world history."

"All right history professor," Mac laughed. "What else should be considered? And don't tell me ye dinnae ken—you don't know."

"Well, since you've opened this can of worms, I'll concede that Hitler is bullheaded enough to invade Poland for several reasons," Gray continued. "First of all, he believes he would be successful even if he faces opposition. He reasons he could overrun Polish armed forces quickly and easily with his superior weaponry and manpower. In addition, he considers the British and French leaders, Neville Chamberlain and Edouard Daladier, to be weak sisters. Chamberlain and Daladier would prefer peace negotiations and settlements at nearly any cost rather than going to war."

McLeod broke into applause.

"I knew I chose the right man to head our school," he said. "You're knowledgeable, persuasive and a critical thinker. And, a damn good communicator. You've confirmed my belief that you're the man I need."

Puzzled, Graham sat back in his chair.

"What are you getting at, Mac? I know you didn't ask me here to discuss international politics."

MacLeod placed both hands on the table and leaned forward.

"I want you for another job. I'm being reassigned to Pittsburgh to head up a production team that will oversee increased turnout and speedier delivery of coal from our mines. I want you on that team as my right hand.

"The company firmly believes that a world war is coming and that America will be pulled into it. What this means is an all-out effort to produce more coal to fuel the energy needs. Bituminous coal, like Selkirk mines in eastern Kentucky, supplies more energy than any other fuels used in America. So this means our coal will be more in demand.

"This also means we have to keep our experienced miners on the job. Our Selkirk experts believe we'll have a lot of volunteers for service if this country goes to war. They also speculate we could have a selective service draft. We'll have to convince the government to let us keep our people on the job and get them a military deferment. Deferments should be given for those in jobs of essential service.

"You've got a wife and a son," Mac continued, "and if you leave to fight, who would care for them? Coal mining is an essential service and, if you join us, we'd have to get you deferred. But, believe me, you'd earn it. You'd be in service for defense purposes, serving your country from the home front."

Gray rubbed his chin and smiled.

"You've become quite an orator and a pretty good salesman. I'll have to think about it. I'll wait for an offer I can't refuse."

"The added benefit is the income," Mac said. "You'd be making a lot more as a defense specialist than you would as a schoolteacher. Go ahead, think about it. But don't wait too long. I'll be leaving for Pittsburgh next month and I'll be back to make a formal offer."

The summer of 1939 meant a return to graduate school for Graham. He already was working on his dissertation and had only one more class to complete. With luck, he would meet his masters' degree requirements by the end of August.

Martha had her ear glued to the radio when he returned home. She held up her hand for silence as she turned up the volume.

German Chancellor and Nazi Party leader Adolf Hitler has reportedly delayed an invasion of Poland in view of a treaty of mutual assistance signed today between Great Britain and the Polish nation. The treaty supersedes a previous temporary agreement between the two European countries. It is reported, however, that Hitler is ignoring diplomatic efforts to further restrain his invasion intentions.

"This doesn't sound good, Gray," Martha commented as she turned off the radio. "If there's a war in Europe, we could be dragged into it. What will this mean for us—I mean you, me and Jack?"

"Probably nothing," Gray responded as he wrestled with his son. Jack cackled as his father tickled his stomach.

"America wants no part of a war in Europe and it's going to take a lot to get us involved. Let's not be all gloom and doom about it."

A week later, however, Gray had second thoughts. Hitler began hostilities in Poland and, in response, Great Britain and France declared war on Germany.

World War II had begun.

CHAPTER THIRTY-FIVE

THE ATTACK

Charley Fitzpatrick threw the newspaper on Gray Graham's desk. "Have you seen this?" he asked.

The front-page headline read:

Selective Service Act Signed.

The deck underneath declared:

All Men Ages 21-45
Required To Register
For Nation's First
Peacetime Draft

The story revealed that the Selective Service System would serve as an independent agency to identify and induct eligible men for military service. It noted that the act, signed into law by President Franklin Roosevelt, was initiated due to "rising world conflicts."

"We're preparing for war," Gray announced. "We'll wait now for the other shoe to drop. I wonder what it will take to get us in it?"

Charley shrugged.

"It won't take much," he said. "If some country steps on our toes, Washington won't cry 'ouch,' it'll push back, hard.

"At the very least, you have some fresh material to liven up your history classes," Fitzpatrick joked.

The 1940 school year had the Citation school faculty looking over its shoulders. Men and women alike wondered not if, but when the military draft would begin. America was edging closer to becoming involved, despite President Roosevelt's declaration that he would not send troops into any foreign war.

Germany, meanwhile, invaded five European countries before taking control of France. And the German Luftwaffe used its air superiority to bomb London unmercifully. Privately, Gray took notice, wrestling with what courses of action he should take. He still had not received a formal offer from Selkirk and McLeod, and the time frame for draft registration was upon him. America was just a step away from being drawn into the conflict, but Gray felt he was two steps behind.

But, he wasn't alone. Charley was concerned he could be called up before finding a support solution for his family. And, the distaff faculty worried what their fates might be if their husbands were called. It was a new decade filled with unrest.

Graham trudged along the rail tracks as he made his way home. His mind was filled with what was happening and what might happen where the war in Europe was concerned. Charley had joked that he had at least some fresh material for his history classes, but Gray and Charley both knew that the war and its future for America was no laughing matter. And neither was the surprise beyond his apartment door.

Martha sat on the sofa with an arm around Jack's shoulders. Sitting opposite her was Liam McLeod.

"Mac, what are you doing here?" the startled Gray cried.

"Sit down, Gray," Martha said. "You told Mr. McLeod you were waiting for an offer you couldn't refuse. He's been telling us about it."

Graham glanced from Martha and Jack to McLeod. No one spoke, and the silence was deafening. Gray reached for a chair.

"I think I'd better hear this sitting down," he said.

Mac had several papers in his hands and he handed one to Gray.

"This is a contract with Selkirk Mining that has your name on it. Your title will be Assistant Production Manager and your salary will be $2,400 a year. That's $700 more than the average salary in this country and considerably more than you're making as a principal and schoolteacher.

"You'll live in a two-bedroom house provided by Selkirk. It's rent free and has a yard for Jack to play in. We need you in Pittsburgh the first week of October. You'll be my right hand, reporting directly to me. Martha and I have talked at length about this opportunity and she agrees if you agree."

Gray looked at Martha and she nodded her approval.

"Here's a pen," Mac announced. "Sign at the bottom."

Reluctantly, Graham took the pen and took his time reading the contract. It was as good as advertised.

"But we've just started the school year," Gray mildly protested. "They can't find a replacement this quick."

"What about Charley Fitzpatrick?" McLeod asked. "He has a wife and two children. If there's a draft, he likely will be exempted. Or, at worst, not called up for quite a while."

Graham looked again at the contract.

"Twenty-four hundred and a yard for Jack. We could even afford a new coat and a new dress for my wife."

He looked again at Martha who smiled and mouthed, 'Sign it.' And, he did.

Charley accepted Gray's position at the school and the goodbyes were filled with emotion. The move to Pittsburgh went smoothly and the house in nearby McKeesport was impressive. And, as Mac anticipated, Graham was an immediate success in his new job. He and Mac attacked coal production with a fury, and Selkirk was a top U.S. producer as 1940 came to a close.

War news notwithstanding, one of the most exciting events of 1941 had to do with baseball. Boston outfielder Ted Williams ended the American League season with a .406 batting average. The most alarming news, however, would take place less than three months later.

The Grahams had finished a Sunday afternoon snack when the news flash came over the radio.

> *Today, at 7:55 a.m. Hawaii time, Japan launched a surprise attack on the naval base at Pearl Harbor. Details of the attack on the Oahu Island are scarce, but untold damage to the U.S. Pacific Fleet is reported.*
>
> *According to initial reports, Japanese bombers and torpedo-carrying planes attacked warships, aircraft and military installations. The raid in Hawaii occurred while Japanese officials were negotiating in Washington with U.S. Secretary of State Cordell Hull.*

Gray quickly turned the dial for additional reports. There was no shortage of coverage.

With its attack, Japan has declared war on the United States and Great Britain. President Roosevelt is in the process of mobilizing all U.S. forces and is expected to ask Congress tomorrow for a declaration of war with Japan.

The attack came in two waves, with six battleships sunk and 112 other vessels either sunk or damaged. Some 160 aircraft also have been destroyed.

Washington sources also report that Germany and Italy are expected to declare war on the U.S. within hours.

The news was breaking fast, and what information one station didn't have another did. Gray and Martha listened in wordless shock.

The attack is said to have been launched from two aircraft carriers. It has also been learned that U.S. forces have downed six Japanese planes and sunk four submarines. American losses, however, are severe and casualties are expected to be in the thousands.

Gray was exhausted and Martha was in tears. One of her brothers was in the Navy and another was a marine. And one of them was stationed in Hawaii. She frantically kept trying to call home, but the phone lines were flooded.

America was at war, and everyone knew it.

CHAPTER THIRTY-SIX

BACK TO REALITY

Spring 1990
The narrative concludes

"That's quite a story," I remarked. "I can recall bits and pieces, but had no idea what you and Mom experienced.

"I remember the war years and I remember when we moved back to Kentucky. That's when you returned to teaching."

Dad took two more pills and washed them down with a thermos filled with water.

"When I left Selkirk in forty-six everything was different," he said. "The war was over, the economy had recovered and many of the mines had played out, Citation included. Selkirk was in the process of leaving Citation when I decided to go back to teaching. The company sold its houses and equipment and the school was turned over to the county."

"I bet that made Jack Nixon happy," I commented.

Dad laughed.

"No, Nixon had other problems. His past caught up with him and he was sent to prison. The state police got involved in the shooting with the Brushy Fork police chief, and Nixon was convicted of the murder of Nathan Sherman. That and his bootleg coal and moonshining operations were his undoing."

Dad took a final look and patted the stone on which he sat.

"Where I'm sitting is about where the school steps were located. You'd never know there once was a schoolhouse here. Nostalgia is great and nothing can ever replace the memories, but in the end, nature is the ultimate winner. As soon as we leave it takes over."

Dad looked to the hills and smiled. Darnell Bowman didn't know what Dad was looking for, but said he hoped he wouldn't be disappointed. He wasn't.

"Let's head back," I suggested. "I need to stop at the store and get some gas."

Just beyond the double doors at Trivette Enterprises was a promotional sign. The top line read in bold letters, "**We Sell the Necessities of Life**." Underneath, in smaller letters, a line read, "*Food, Clothing and Shelter*." I did a double take, but Dad didn't seem to notice.

I walked to the counter while Dad continued to look at the merchandise.

"I need to fill up my car," I said. "Do I need to make a deposit first?"

"No, not at all," the proprietor said. "We'll figure out what you owe when you come back inside. Just let me know how many gallons you pumped."

When I returned, I pulled out my wallet and addressed the clerk. He was tall, well built and friendly.

"You sure are a trusting soul," I grinned. "I could have filled up and taken off."

"No, you wouldn't do that," he laughed. "I trust my customers and know most of them personally. But I haven't seen you before."

He reached out his hand to shake mine.

"I'm James Trivette. Welcome to Trivette Enterprises."

"I'm Jack Graham."

James cocked his head and frowned.

"Graham," he mused. "There used to be a family of Grahams here before the war. One of them was the school principal."

"That would be my father," I said.

Trivette burst into laughter and pumped my hand.

"What about that!" he exclaimed. "Your daddy was a big man around here. He influenced a lot of students, including my dad. Did you see the sign when you came in? My father was J.D. Trivette. He bought this store when Selkirk Mining left and one of the first things he did was to put up that sign. He said its message changed his life."

"Yeah, I've heard the story."

"He told us—I mean my brother, my sister and me—that Mr. Graham taught him that food, clothing and shelter were the basic necessities of life. That you used them as your foundation to do good things and build a better life."

"I'm guessing that it worked," I remarked.

"Absolutely! Dad pushed us to get an education and make something of ourselves. Russell, my brother, went to law school and is an attorney in Louisville and my sister, Susan, is a teacher in Owensboro. I went to community college and decided I wanted to own my own business. I took over the store after Dad died and used it as a base for my construction business. We already were selling groceries and clothing, and I expanded it to include a good line of hardware. I've built homes and buildings throughout Eastern Kentucky and Trivette Enterprises has turned out to be pretty successful."

"Your father must have been quite a man," I remarked. "I understand he was killed during Korea."

"Yeah, but he left Russell, Susan and me with a great heritage. Dad said he was a slow learner, but, thanks to your father, he said he learned to believe in himself. He taught us that great things are possible if we work hard and apply ourselves.

"He also was a great patriot. He believed in America and the opportunities it provided a coal-mining kid who, he said, came from nothing. He had no hesitation about fighting for his country."

Trivette cleared his throat and blew his nose.

"Sorry," he said. "I sometimes get emotional when I think what my dad did for us."

"I know what you mean," I responded. "My father always has been an inspiration for me."

James took my cash and counted out some change.

"Is your father still alive?" he inquired.

"Funny you should ask," I said. "He's standing over there."

Dad was talking with a clerk. James left the counter and we walked over to my father.

"Dad, this is James Trivette," I introduced. "He's J.D. Trivette's son and is the owner of the store."

James shook Dad's hand and embraced him in a bear hug.

"Wow!" he said. "This is a real pleasure. I never thought I'd meet the man who had such a major influence on my family. How are you, sir?"

"I'm fine," he lied. "And, look at you! You look like your dad. Jimmy Dan must have been really proud of you."

James stepped back and pointed at the sign.

"You know where that came from," he smiled. "Dad said you would whirl around, point at him, and ask what were the necessities of life."

Dad laughed.

"Finally, all I had to do was point. Jimmy Dan never missed a beat."

"Dad said you also were pretty tough. He told me that you earned his crowd's respect, but they always were a little afraid of you. You had the reputation of being 'Hell on Wheels.'"

"We had a great group of students at Citation," Dad commented. "We had our disagreements, but their hearts were in the right place. I'll never forget them."

We turned to leave, but Dad stopped, whirled and pointed a finger at Trivette.

James smiled and shouted, "Food, clothing and shelter!"

CHAPTER THIRTY-SEVEN

EXIT

It was late spring, not quite warm enough for short sleeves, but the hills and valleys around Citation already were green. It was a sunny day with blue skies and the natural beauty of the Eastern Kentucky mountains was magnificent.

We pulled away from Trivette's store and toward what had been the entrance to Citation's main street. I instinctively stopped when I reached the railroad tracks.

"Why are you stopping?" Dad inquired.

I felt foolish. The track hadn't connected to the main line in decades.

"Don't want to get hit by a coal train," I murmured.

"I think you missed it by about forty years," he replied.

He wasn't smiling, but his eyes expressed delight at catching me off guard.

I drove through the valley and up a steep hill that led toward the junction. Nothing was said, but I could tell Dad was uneasy. The pain was coming back.

"That was interesting and a real surprise," I commented. "Trivette Enterprises, I mean. Despite what Darnell Bowman said, I had no idea that James Trivette could have developed such a thriving business in an abandoned coal camp. You must have made quite an impression on Jimmy Dan. He certainly made sure his offspring were beneficiaries."

I looked at Dad, but he didn't respond.

"That sign in the store really was something," I continued. "I guess the necessities of life lesson was a real breakthrough for Jimmy Dan. What you taught him became a philosophy of life, not to mention a good merchandising technique."

I paused, but there was no response.

"Funny how something as simple as that could be passed down to another generation and make such a good impression," I added. "A lawyer, a teacher and an entrepreneur—all because of one thing."

Dad fumbled in a pocket for the brown vial, the prescription that Dr. Hashmeer had written. The last few hours had been physically trying. He was breathing harder and beads of perspiration flecked across his forehead. He shook three pills into his other hand and washed them down with a few gulps of water from the thermos.

He sighed quietly and settled back in the seat. The medicine was beginning to take effect. Dad was taking it more often and in greater quantities, something that Hashmeer urged him to do as the frequency and intensity of the pain increased.

"Well, aren't you impressed?" I asked. "I know I would be. I think it's great that a teacher could make such a difference."

Dad reached for the dashboard, pushed against it and repositioned himself.

"Like the man said," he smiled. "I was Hell on Wheels."

I didn't realize Dad had heard James' last remarks. I thought for a moment about what we'd experienced in the past few days. We'd visited a coal operation, a town and a school that no longer were there. But the memories were. And I had seen it vividly through Dad's eyes.

Through him, I'd learned things about Citation that I could never have known when I lived there as a preschooler. Citation was about hard times, trying times and survival. It was about living on the edge, heartaches and trying to make something out of little or nothing. And about some people who'd made a difference.

"Hell on Wheels, huh?" I grinned as I gave Dad a quick look. "Maybe James is on to something."

Dad was breathing easily, and the medication had provided a burst of energy.

"Thanks, Jack," he said. "I appreciate you making this trip for me. I've thought a lot about Citation since your mother died and I wanted to see it one last time. Despite the economic struggles and the threat of war, in some ways the years here were the best of times. There were a lot of good people, and we fought through the hard times together."

"I vaguely remember some of the people," I said, "and I remember sitting in the back of the classroom when Mom was substitute teaching.

She told me to sit still and be quiet and, if I paid attention, I might learn something.

"One person I remember was Mr. Fitzpatrick. He would joke with me and sometimes we would talk when a class was over. He did this one thing I'll never forget. He'd become very serious and look at one side of my face and then the other. Then, he'd say, 'Jack, I don't believe you shaved this morning.' I'd tell him I didn't shave and he'd shake his head. 'You'd better shave or your wife is going to get upset. You are married aren't you?'

"I'd tell him no and he'd look surprised. He was a lot of fun. Do you know where he is now?"

"Charley was the principal at Citation until the school was turned over to the county. He and his family moved to Indiana, and I believe he served one or two years in the Army. I haven't seen or heard from him in years."

"Mom used to talk about Eileen Branscomb, the nurse who was her close friend. How did things turn out for her?"

"Martha kept in touch with Eileen and met with her several times in Lexington after the war. When she left Citation, Eileen moved in with her parents in Ashland, had her baby and resumed her nursing career.

"She had a boy and Martha said he looked like Boyd Palmer, but had a personality like Eileen's father. The boy turned out really well. He went to medical school and specialized in obstetrics. The last I heard, he was delivering babies in Louisville."

"What about Liam McLeod?"

"Ahhh, old Mac!" Dad exclaimed. "I think he hired me because of my name. He said I was as much a Scotsman as he was. When he totally agreed with me about something he'd slap his knee and say, 'Ay, laddie, there's still a bit of the old country in you!'

"Mac once asked me how I liked living in Pittsburgh, and I said you and your mother would like to make the area a permanent home. But, I didn't. I said Kentucky was home and some day we'd return. 'Ay, you miss the mountains of your heritage,' he said. 'Your clan embraces the hill country as much as it embraces you.'

"Mac lived with his family in Pittsburgh after he retired. I was notified of his death in fifty six and went back for his funeral. I never saw so many fair-haired blue-eyed people."

I remembered when Fred Burden was wounded in a shootout and saw him carried into the company infirmary.

"What ever happened to Fred Burden?" I asked.

Dad shook his head.

"I have no idea. Charley Fitzpatrick mentioned once that Bernice had resigned her teaching position and that she and Fred had moved. He didn't say where. I was always glad that Fred was on my side. I sure would have hated to have him as an enemy."

Dad chuckled as he focused on Fred.

"If there ever was someone who was Hell on Wheels it was Fred," he stated.

Dad sighed and leaned back, his head resting atop the seat.

"I'm worn out, Jack. As the saying goes, 'I've been rode hard and put up wet.' It's been a journey, but I wouldn't have missed it for the world."

We were nearing the junction with the interstate. Once on I-75, there would be some rest stops where we could take a break. Dad's eyes were closed and he already was resting.

"Let's stop off for some coffee," I said. "I sure could use some, how about you?"

The traffic was heavy, and I kept my eyes on the road. I moved into the right lane preparing to exit.

"That sound okay to you?" I asked.

Dad's eyes remained closed and he didn't reply right away. When he did, he spoke in a gravelly tone.

"Let's do it. Maybe that'll perk me up."

CHAPTER THIRTY-EIGHT

THE LAST MILE

I wheeled onto an off ramp after seeing a golden arches sign and found a parking spot near the restaurant's front door. I didn't have an opportunity to get Dad's door. He was out of the car and stretching by the time I got there.

I asked the waitress for some coffee and apple pie and Dad, viewing her nametag, told Sarah to make it two, with one caveat.

"I'd like some truck driver coffee," he said, "and, Sarah, bet I don't have to tell you what that is."

"Hot, strong and black," she smiled. "Coming right up."

The pie was good and the coffee hit the spot, at least mine did. I wondered if Dad's brew was up to par, and so did Sarah. She stood clasping the tray to her bosom after asking for his reaction.

"Not bad," he said. "Did you run a dirty sock through it?"

"Didn't have to," she laughed. "We double brewed it and stirred it with a spoon. When the spoon melted, I knew we were on the right track."

Dad grinned and raised his cup in a toast.

"You're okay, Sarah. You deserve a healthy tip."

"If you survive a second cup, I'll take it," she winked.

Dad took another sip as Sarah left.

"I may adopt that girl," he deadpanned.

The break was good for both of us. I was refreshed and Dad had rallied. He leaned back against the booth cushion as he posed the question.

"What did you really think of Pittsburgh?" he asked. "I don't believe we ever talked about it."

We had lived in the Steel City region for six years. I started school in McKeesport and was in the sixth grade when we moved back to Kentucky.

"I liked it," I replied. "But I wondered sometimes if the sun would ever shine on the city. It was so smoky and dirty downtown. McKeesport wasn't a lot better, but I have a lot of good memories about the town and the people."

"It was always dark in downtown Pittsburgh," Dad agreed. "At mid-morning the streetlights would still be on. The soot, smog and smoke from coal fumes and the steel mills dominated. I remember the mayor saying we could complain later, but 'right now, we've got a war to win.'"

"Do you remember me talking about Jimmy Krakowski?" I asked.

"Was he your friend in that air raid warden group? He also might have been the one to create all that stir about Japanese planes flying over Allegheny County."

"Yeah, he's the one. When I was in the second grade they signed us up to serve as Junior Air Raid Wardens. They gave us a white shoulder cross belt, a badge and a red tin helmet along with a silhouette chart of enemy airplanes. We were told to memorize the chart and study any aircraft flying over the county.

"Jimmy was all excited at school one day, claiming he had seen a Japanese Zero. Word got around school and the principal had Jimmy explain in detail what he had seen. Some police officers and a Civil Defense specialist got involved and they took Jimmy to the airport for more questioning. While he was there, he pointed to a plane taxing down the runway and said, 'That's it!'

"It turned out to be an Army trainer that was flying low-level practice runs. After that, our group concentrated on assisting with scrap drives and promoting the sale of war bonds."

"War bonds…we bought as many as we could afford," Dad recalled. "I remember also urging you to save money to buy civil defense stamps."

I smiled as the recollection surfaced.

"The stamps only cost ten cents and you could trade them in to buy War Bonds. You also gave me a cardboard with slots for seventy-five quarters. When it was full I turned it in to the post office for a $25 war bond. I bought my first bicycle when that bond matured."

I was on a memory roll. The next thought was about baseball.

"Do you remember that one-armed outfielder who played for Pittsburgh?"

Dad laughed.

"Yeah, that was Pete Gray. It was toward the end of the war when we went to Forbes Field and I remember you tugging at my arm to look at a player with one arm. We both were amazed when Pete cut off a hit to left. In one quick motion, he fielded the ball, removed his glove and flipped the ball to his throwing hand."

"And I remember him getting a hit," I added. "He was really something. With most players in the service, he got his chance to play in the big leagues."

"And made the most of it," Dad added.

We finished our pie and Dad motioned to Sarah for a second cup of coffee. She poured it with a giggle.

"I just won a quarter," she said. "The cook bet me you wouldn't ask for a second cup."

"What if I ask for a third cup?"

"Just give me time to raise the bet to fifty cents," she smirked.

The coffee break gave Dad a lift, but I could tell he was getting tired.

"You were on the road a lot during the war years," I commented.

"I felt like I spent more time on trains than anything else," Dad observed. "About once a month, I'd travel through West Virginia and Kentucky to visit Selkirk's mines. I never was in Citation long enough to visit with the folks we knew. A good many were in the service and there were a lot of new faces. But every mine was fully staffed and production was at an all-time high.

"The demand for coal was tremendous. I recall 1944 as one of the peak years. In that year alone, Kentucky produced more than 72 million tons and our mines were among the leaders. A fellow named Bill Collins was the manager at Citation, and he told me at the rate they were going there wouldn't be a bucket of coal left in two years. He wasn't far wrong. Citation was played out by 1949."

"Is it fair to say that Kentucky coal helped win the war?" I asked.

"Absolutely," Dad replied. "I can still recall many of the production figures and the part coal had in it. In the last year of the war, the U.S. produced nearly 70 percent of the world's pig iron and more than 70 percent of the steel. Coal fueled that effort and the mass production of battlefield materials was what won the war."

I questioned that statement.

"I'd think it was the service men and women who won the war."

"Listen to this," Dad replied. "I talked with a wounded veteran who operated a machine gun following the Normandy invasion. He said he shot .50 caliber rounds until the barrel overheated and quit. But all he had to do was pull out another barrel and keep firing. That was an option he had that his German counterparts didn't."

I stood up to leave, and Dad struggled a bit as he got to his feet. He caught Sarah's eye and pointed to his cup. She came and delivered another refill. Dad took a final sip and saw the cook raise his hands in defeat. He took out a $10 bill and handed it to Sarah.

"This and that extra fifty cents you just won should buy you more than a cup of truck driver coffee."

Sarah kissed Dad's cheek.

"Will you come back to see me?" she asked. "I'll serve you anytime."

"I'll do my best," he said.

I took Dad's arm as we headed to the car. He staggered a bit and his face had a gray pallor. His breathing was heavier as I slid behind the wheel.

"Maybe you should take some more pills," I suggested, handing him the thermos of water.

He nodded and removed two pills from the brown vial. He washed them down and shook out two others. This was the first time he had taken that many.

"You okay?" I asked.

"I'm really tired," he murmured. "It's been a long journey."

I started the car and made it back to the interstate before taking a quick glance. His head was resting atop the seat and the still open bottle of pills was in his left hand. His fingers relaxed and the bottle of pills slipped from his hand and onto the floor.

His journey had ended.

EPILOGUE

The Necessities of Life is based in a fictional community in Southeastern Kentucky. The community, Citation, is not unlike many coal mining towns formed in Southern Appalachia. There were a number of reputable companies that built good communities and took care of the inhabitants, their employees. But, you don't always hear about them.

Some of coal towns were extremely rough and lacking in basic needs and services, as the companies that formed and ran them were only interested in the bottom dollar. Stereotyped and often more sensational accounts depict coal country as filled with poorly educated, starving, out-of-luck families who owed their lives to the company store. A "Grapes of Wrath" existence is believed to evoke more emotion and greater readership.

This story, although fictionalized, is based on fact. Such places as Citation actually existed. Because of the largely Scots-Irish heritage of those inhabitants of Eastern Kentucky and its coal towns, there were and are some common traits. For example, as reflected in the book's characters, the people are deeply loyal to family and friends. They have a quick temper and tend to take matters into their own hands when family and friends are wronged. Justice is paramount. They're also suspicious of those in official capacities, particularly ones who want to tell them what to do and how to do it.

In coal communities like Citation, it wasn't unusual for male residents to carry a weapon or weapons. A .38-caliber revolver was a popular side arm and those who carried knew how to use them.

The Necessities of Life is a realistic portrayal of the Eastern Kentucky residents who experienced the coal industry during the Great Depression.

It also is a story about the value of education and educators who struggled to make a difference. Protagonist Gray Graham and his school's faculty are characterizations of those individuals who were and are dedicated to improving lives and conditions in the region.

Bernice Burden says it best in Chapter 22, "The Candidate." She notes that education is about accepting students just as they are and working with them to make them the best they can be.

"Their success," she concludes, "is our success."

ABOUT THE AUTHOR

Ed Ford is an author of historical fiction and has written five books, two plays and a number of articles about the U.S. Civil War and other historical activities in his home state of Kentucky.

Prior to his career as a novelist, Ford was an award-winning corporate editor and public relations specialist with Ford Motor and The Goodyear Tire & Rubber Companies, and was a newspaper and magazine reporter and editor.

The University of Kentucky journalism graduate operates his own public relations firm in Richmond, Kentucky, and has served as public relations director for Berea College.